"Come On," Donna Urged. "Tell Me. I Can Handle It."

"I'm sure you can," Marty replied, cupping her shoulders with his hands. Dipping his head, he kissed her brow, nose and mouth. The first two kisses were light. The third bordered on lusty.

"Marty..." Donna moaned when he finally released her.

"I'm sorry, but my lips are sealed about the outcome of the Murphy's Law cliffhanger. So if you'll excuse me, sweetheart..."

Marty grinned to himself as he anticipated a satisfying conclusion to this skirmish between the sexes. Donna had forced his hand when she'd threatened to use "fiendishly erotic techniques" to obtain the information she was seeking. After all, he'd been on the verge of admitting what he did— and didn't—know about the conclusion when she'd issued her ultimatum.

Bring on the fiendishly erotic techniques, sweetheart, he thought. *Because I'm going to keep my mouth shut as long as I can....*

Dear Reader:

What makes a Silhouette Desire hero? This is a question I often ask myself—it's part of my job to think about these things!—and I *know* it's something you all think about, too. I like my heroes rugged, sexy and sometimes a little infuriating. I love the way our heroes are sometimes just a little bit in the dark about love . . . *and* about what makes the heroine "tick." It's all part of their irresistible charm.

This March, I want you all to take a good look at our heroes and—if you want—let me know what you think about them!

Naturally, we have a *Man of the Month* who just can't be beat—Dane Lassiter in Diana Palmer's *The Case of the Mesmerizing Boss.* This story is doubly good because not only is it a *Man of the Month* title, it's also the first book in Diana Palmer's new *series,* called MOST WANTED. As for Lassiter, he's a hero you're not likely to ever forget.

Do you think playboys can be tamed? I certainly do! And you can watch one really get his comeuppance in Linda Turner's delightful *Philly and the Playboy.* Barbara McCauley creates a sexy, mountain man (is there any other kind?) in *Man From Cougar Pass,* and Carole Buck brings us a hero who's a bit more citified—but no less intriguing—in *Knight and Day.* And if a seafaring fellow is the type for you, don't miss Donna Carlisle's *Cast Adrift.*

Some heroes—like some real-life men—are less than perfect, and I have to admit I had a few doubts about Lass Small's *Dominic.* But so many of you wrote in asking for his story that I began to wonder if Dominic shouldn't have equal time to state his case. (You'll remember he gave Tate Lambert such a hard time in *Goldilocks and the Behr.*) Is Dominic a hero? I think he very well might be, but I'm interested in hearing what you all thought about this newly tamed man.

So, I've said all I have to say *except* that I do wish you best wishes for happy reading. Now I'm waiting to hear from you.

Until next month,

Lucia Macro
Senior Editor

CAROLE BUCK

KNIGHT AND DAY

SILHOUETTE *Desire*®

Published by Silhouette Books New York

America's Publisher of Contemporary Romance

SILHOUETTE BOOKS
300 East 42nd St., New York, N.Y. 10017

KNIGHT AND DAY

Copyright © 1992 by Carol Buckland

All rights reserved. Except for use in any review, the reproduction or utilization of this work in whole or in part in any form by any electronic, mechanical or other means, now known or hereafter invented, including xerography, photocopying and recording, or in any information storage or retrieval system, is forbidden without the permission of the publisher, Silhouette Books, 300 E. 42nd St., New York, N.Y. 10017

ISBN: 0-373-05699-0

First Silhouette Books printing March 1992

Printed in the U.S.A.

Books by Carole Buck

Silhouette Desire

Time Enough for Love #565
Paradise Remembered #614
White Lace Promises #644
Red-Hot Satin #677
Knight and Day #699

Silhouette Romance

Make-believe Marriage #752

CAROLE BUCK

is a television news writer and movie reviewer who lives in Atlanta. She is single. Her hobbies include cake decorating, ballet and traveling. She collects frogs, but does not kiss them. Carole says she's in love with life. She hopes the books she writes reflect this.

One

───

It was love at first laugh—or pretty close. But Marty Knight didn't figure that out until much later.

Love was probably the last thing on Marty's mind as he stood center stage at The Funny Farm, one of Los Angeles' best-known comedy clubs. In point of fact, love was probably the last thing on his mind when he stood—or sat or sprawled—just about anywhere.

Martin "Marty" Knight was perfectly willing to admit that he was no expert when it came to love. Hell, he was willing to admit that he'd need a lot more experience before he'd even qualify as an amateur at the emotion! But when it came to *laughs,* he was a connoisseur. An afficionado. He had to be. He was a professional comedian. Laughter was his livelihood.

Giggles and guffaws.

Chuckles and chortles.

Big, braying ha-ha-has and tiny, tittering tee-hee-hees.

Marty wasn't picky about the exact sound or style. He just wanted—no, he absolutely *needed*—to hear people laugh and to know his humor had inspired them to do so.

He'd been seven when he'd discovered that he had a
knack for saying funny things—and for saying things funny.
Even now, twenty-four years later, there was no way he
could fully articulate the impact of that discovery. How
could he explain that suddenly he'd felt good—really, truly
good—about himself and the world around him?

Of course the feeling hadn't lasted very long. Not then,
and not on any of the countless occasions when he'd been
able to recapture it by making somebody laugh. Deep in his
heart, Marty believed there might come a day when it *would*
last. But until that day arrived...

Marty recognized how much he depended on laughter. In
a sense, he was addicted to it. Still, if he had to go through
life hooked on something, he figured he could do a whole
hell of a lot worse than humor.

Marty first heard the laugh that stole his heart while loi-
tering at The Funny Farm's bar, waiting to take his turn in
the spotlight. He'd dropped in at the club about thirty minutes before, hoping to unwind after a long day of taping
Murphy's Law, the television comedy that had made him a
household name.

At first, the prospects for unwinding hadn't seemed very
good. No sooner had Marty settled himself on a stool and
accepted a glass of ginger ale from one of the bartenders
than he'd been accosted by several autograph seekers. He'd
smiled impersonally, signed illegibly, and sent them on their
way. Next had been an encounter with an old acquaintance
who'd taken it as a personal insult that he hadn't wanted to
guzzle beer and reminisce about their shared experiences on
the comedy circuit. That little episode had been followed by
an extremely unwelcome have-I-got-a-script-for-you pitch
from an obnoxious, and highly successful, agent named
Barry Cooperman.

Marty had been on the verge of telling Cooperman to
shove it when Zeke Peters, the owner of The Funny Farm,
had wandered over and done the job for him. He'd mentally added that favor to the long, long list of favors he owed
the older man.

Zeke Peters was a great, gray-haired hulk of a man in his
late fifties. He was profane and unpredictable. He was also

the closest thing Los Angeles had to a patron saint of stand-up comics.

Zeke occupied a very special spot in Marty's life. He was a friend. He was also the person who'd helped Marty stay grounded during the disorienting period when his career had taken off and gone ballistic.

After some casual chitchat, Zeke had suggested that Marty might like to take the mike once The Funny Farm's current headliner finished his act. Marty had instantly agreed. It had been a couple of weeks since he'd performed in front of a club audience and he knew he was in need of the jolt that only a stand-up could give him.

He'd frankly admitted as much to Zeke.

"Yeah, I thought so," the older man had grunted, scratching his bearded chin. Then, without further ado, he'd ambled away to make the necessary arrangements for Marty's appearance.

Marty heard "the laugh" less than a minute later.

It came floating back to him from the front of the club. It was feminine. Very, very feminine. Provocative, yet oddly pure. It was also slightly out of sync with the laughter from the rest of the audience.

The joke that had apparently prompted it had been a subtle one. The laughing woman—whomever she was—had evidently "gotten" the punch line a fraction of a second before anyone else in the club...except maybe Marty.

Somebody in the business? he wondered, cocking his head as his pulse gave an odd little kick. A professional, maybe?

The comic on stage told another offbeat joke. Again, Marty heard the laugh. No. More than that. This time he *felt* it, clear down to the soles of his feet.

He shifted his weight on the bar stool.

He took a deep gulp of his ginger ale.

He kept on listening.

Not a pro, Marty decided, rejecting the notion that the source of the lilting laughter was another comic. The sound was too open for that. It was too appreciative.

Oh, sure, comics laughed at other comics' material. But Marty knew that when they laughed because the material was good, there tended to be an undercurrent of envy or anger. And when they laughed because the material was bad...

Marty shook his head. He'd been on the receiving end of that kind of merciless, on-stage humiliation only once. It hadn't been the worst thing that ever happened to him, not by a long shot. Still, he'd made damned sure it never happened again.

There was nothing harmful in the laughter coming from somewhere amid the row of tables set up directly in front of The Funny Farm's small stage. Quite the contrary. This was healthy laughter. Heartfelt. All in all, it was just about the most perfect sound Marty Knight had ever heard.

The only thing wrong with it was that it wasn't *his* laughter. It belonged to the comic who was up on the stage, telling the jokes.

Marty shifted his weight again, conscious that his snug-fitting black denim jeans were fitting more snugly with each passing moment. He swallowed the remainder of his ginger ale. There was more fizz in his bloodstream than in the carbonated beverage.

Lady, he thought, narrowing his brown eyes and peering toward the front of the club. *I don't know who you are. But before tonight's over, you're going to be laughing for me.*

Marty was on stage about four minutes before he spotted the source behind the laughter that had touched him so potently. It took him that long because he'd made it a point to open his set with very hot material. His aim was to own the audience—the *whole* audience—right away. Once he accomplished that, he could start working one-on-one.

Marty had always come on strong in the spotlight. From the start of his career, he'd been known for his intense, live-wire performances. On the edge, but in control...that's the way he operated when he did stand-up comedy.

Yet before *Murphy's Law* had made him a star—before all the acclaim about his supposed ''comic genius''—he'd had the luxury of being able to build up to his really big laughs if he chose to indulge in it. Becoming an overnight sensation after seven grueling years on the comedy-club circuit had deprived him of that. Marty knew he was now expected to "kill" every time he opened his mouth. Being amusing at regular intervals wasn't good enough. He had to be absolutely hilarious from start to finish.

He hit The Funny Farm audience with a quick series of one-liners about contemporary male-female relations. The capper was a double entendre that would have given a TV censor fits.

The audience roared.

Marty scanned the women sitting at the tables arranged nearest the stage. Which one is she? he wondered.

There were three stunning blondes positioned directly in front of him. They were tanned. Toothy. Twenty-ish. Each one was a living testament to the efficacy of aerobics and orthodontia.

Uh-uh, Marty decided, dismissing the first fair-haired lovely.

No way! he judged, mentally scratching the second.

Mmm...maybe, he mused, detecting a hint of intelligence in the flawlessly featured face of the third. While Marty was acutely aware that there were a lot of intelligent people in the world who lacked the ability to laugh at themselves or anything else, he'd never known a truly stupid individual who had a sense of humor. If the blonde had brains—

Marty realized the initial explosion of laughter he'd detonated was subsiding. He shifted the microphone he was holding from his right hand to his left. After flashing a wicked grin—the grin he'd learned over the years was almost as good for getting him out of trouble as it was for getting him into it—he picked up the thread of his routine. Turning the double entendre he'd uttered a few moments before into a triple one, he proceeded to spin out another string of observations about the fundamental differences between men and women.

The audience howled.

Marty's gaze slid right, homing in on a voluptuous brunette in a skimpy black dress. He eliminated her even more swiftly than he'd eliminated the blondes. While the jewelry she flaunted looked like 14-karat gold, her laugh was brassier than a military band.

Damn! he thought, thrusting the fingers of his right hand back through his dark brown hair. Where *is* she?

Marty decided it was time to throttle down and throw the crowd a curve. He knew he'd successfully established his comic credentials. He'd given his fans the boffo material they expected to hear and he'd "proven" he didn't need a prerecorded laugh track to lay people in the aisles. Now he could move into chancier territory. He could start improvising. Experimenting. He could teach some old gags new tricks.

The first two jokes he told paid off perfectly. Bingo. Bull's-eye. Dead on target.

The third one missed a bit. The fourth went so wide of the mark people actually groaned. Marty redeemed the situation with a quick self-deprecating comment. While the audience was applauding his recovery, he made a rueful quip about the dangers of doing comedy. It was a throwaway line, but it cut close to the bone. Marty knew it was the most personal thing he'd said in public in a long time.

That's when he heard the laugh again.

It came from stage left. It was soft. And sweet. And seductive as hell.

Marty's center of gravity seemed to shift. He started to feel light-headed, as though the blood that was supposed to be nourishing his brain had been rerouted. A pulsing heaviness in his groin made it painfully clear where the blood had gone. He didn't dare look down.

He cracked another joke. It was instinctive. Automatic. The crowd went crazy.

It's all right, Knight, Marty told himself, trying to ignore the insistent throb between his thighs. *It's cool. They like you. They're laughing at your stuff. Nobody's noticing what's going on just below your belt buckle. All you've got to do now is turn your head and take a look at the lady who's got you so torqued up.*

But what if she's an eyesore? he challenged, milking the audience's reaction with a smooth bit of body English.

She won't be, came the confident reply. *No woman with a beautiful laugh is ugly.*

Well, what if she has a husband? What if he's a patho-logically jealous professional football player who doesn't like other men ogling his wife?

You're stalling!

No, I'm not, he argued. The crowd was calming down. It was almost time to stir them up again. *I'm trying to antici-pate—*

Dammit, Knight, if you "anticipate" any more, you're going to humiliate yourself like some horny high school kid. For God's sake, turn your head and look at her!

Marty cracked another joke, garnered another big laugh, then did just that.

He knew her the instant he laid eyes on her. He'd never seen her before in his life, but he knew her nonetheless. The response she evoked in him was visceral. It ran so deep it seemed to stem from the very structure of his DNA.

Her chin-length hair was auburn and rippled around her fair, heart-shaped face like polished silk. Her features were more quirky than classic. Elegant cheekbones and an elfin chin. Wide green eyes set beneath slightly asymmetrical brows. A pertly upturned nose and a lushly passionate mouth.

She was wearing a simple dress of peach-colored jersey. Minimal makeup. No jewelry except a collection of narrow metal bangles on her left wrist. They glinted in the spillover from the lights on the stage.

She wasn't bionically beautiful like the three blondes. She wasn't bountifully bosomed like the brunette, either. Yet she possessed a quality of womanly warmth that made Marty's breath catch at the top of his throat.

There was something radiant about her. He couldn't think of a better word to describe it. The lady glowed like a can-dle flame. To a man who knew from painful, personal ex-perience what it was like to be alone and afraid in the dark, she was irresistible.

She laughed for him once. More than anything else in the world, Marty wanted her to laugh for him again.

When he made another joke, he got what he wanted ... and then some.

* * *

Marty was sweating like a long-distance runner at the end of a marathon when he came off stage nearly an hour later. His heart was thumping and his breath was coming in and out in short, sharp gasps. He was torn between absolute exhilaration and utter exhaustion.

Somebody handed him a towel. He used it to mop his face and neck. Somebody else handed him a paper cup full of water. He drained it in a single greedy gulp.

Out front, he thought. I've got to get out front.

He turned to go and ran head-on into Zeke Peters.

"Marty!" the older man boomed, engulfing him in a rib-threatening bear hug. "You were terrific!"

It took some doing, but Marty managed to extricate himself from his friend's exuberant embrace. "Thanks, Zeke," he said sincerely. "I appreciate it. But I've really got to—"

"Great set, Marty," the club's sound man interrupted, giving a thumbs-up signal.

"Thanks," Marty answered reflexively.

"Do you know how fantastic you were?" Zeke demanded, gesturing expansively. "Do you have any idea how—" he lapsed into X-rated language "—fantastic you were?"

"Zeke, I don't have time for this." Marty had thought making *her* laughter *his* would be enough. But it wasn't. Exactly what would be, he didn't know. He'd start with seeing her again, with finding out her name.

"What do you mean, you don't have time? Kid, you just did sixty minutes of some of the most inspired stand-up stuff I've ever seen! And I've seen just about everything. The comedy vultures are going to be feeding off that routine of yours for—"

"Zeke!" Marty broke in, not understanding the force that was driving him but unable to put the brakes on. "Look, there's somebody I have to see. There's a woman out front. Maybe you noticed her. She had a—"

"A woman?" Zeke pronounced the words as though he'd never heard them before. He looked stunned. Even his beard seemed to bristle with astonishment. "Are you telling me...a *woman?* In all the years I've known you, you've never let a woman—'' He broke off, scrutinizing Marty's face. His eyes narrowed to mere slits. "Is *that* what got into you out there?"

"Yes, dammit!" Even as affirmation exploded out of him, Marty realized he was shaking his head in vehement denial. "No," he amended swiftly. Oh, God, now he was nodding! What was happening to him? "I mean—"

"Go," Zeke ordered succinctly, jerking a thumb toward the exit.

Marty did.

She was gone.

Marty stared at the small wooden table where she'd been sitting. He catalogued the items she'd left behind. An empty glass. A half-eaten bowl of salted peanuts. A crumpled paper napkin bearing The Funny Farm's logo and a small smudge of peach-colored lipstick.

"No," he muttered. "Dammit, no."

He was assailed by a sudden urge to pick up the napkin and take it home with him. He'd actually started to reach forward when—

"Uh, Mr. Knight?"

Feeling like a fool, Marty jerked his hand back and pivoted away from the table.

"Marty," he corrected quietly, staring at the young waiter who'd just addressed him. "It's Marty. Not Mr. Knight."

"Oh, uh, sure, Marty," the waiter responded. He was in his early twenties, very much a California kid with his sun-bleached hair, blue eyes and deep tan. He paused for a moment, then cleared his throat nervously and continued speaking. "I, uh, just wanted to say you did an incredible set tonight. You really cooked."

"Thanks," Marty acknowledged the compliment with a nod, then thrust his hands deep into the pockets of the loose-fitting black linen jacket he was wearing. He glanced around, a bitter sense of disappointment gnawing at his gut. The Funny Farm had shifted into its closing-time mode. The houselights had been turned up and it was last call at the bar for the few customers who'd chosen to stick around until the bitter end.

Did you really think she was going to be out here waiting for you? he asked himself.

Yeah, he admitted honestly after a moment. *I really did.*

She'd noticed him noticing her. Marty was certain of it. And she hadn't minded. He was certain of that, too. In fact, he was willing to swear that her response to him had been as powerful as his had been to her. She'd actually flushed the first time their eyes had met!

They'd connected, he thought. Somehow, some way, they'd connected with each other. So why hadn't she—

"...you anything, Marty?"

Marty started, abruptly realizing that the waiter had been speaking to him. "What?"

"Can I, uh, get you anything?"

Marty shook his head. "No," he refused. "I don't want—" He broke off as he registered what The Funny Farm staffer was doing. "Was this your table tonight?" he demanded sharply.

The waiter froze in the act of retrieving the crumpled napkin with the peach lipstick smear. Obviously unsettled, he stared at Marty warily for several seconds. "Well...yeah," he finally answered.

Marty took a deep breath, warning himself not to get his hopes up. "Do you remember the woman who was sitting here?"

"The woman?" the waiter echoed, furrowing his brow. "Well, uh..."

"Late twenties. Maybe thirty. Slender. Reddish-brown hair. Green eyes. She had an incredible laugh."

"Incredible? You mean, like...weird?"

"No. It was—" Marty paused, searching for the right word. "It was wonderful. Soft. Sexy. Something special. God, you must have heard it!"

The waiter screwed up his face, plainly straining to come up with something. "I don't think I—wait a minute. Wait a minute. Yeah. Yeah! Now it's coming back to me." He beamed triumphantly, displaying two rows of flawless white teeth. "Mineral water and a twist of lime."

Marty blinked. "What?"

"Mineral water and a twist of lime. That's what the woman at this table ordered."

"That's *all* you remember about her?"

The waiter looked abashed. "Uh, well, yeah."

"Did you happen to catch her name?"

"'Fraid not."

"Has she ever been to the club before?"

"Uh, I don't think so. I mean, not since I've been here." The waiter heaved a sigh. "I'm sorry, Marty. Really sorry."

"Yeah," Marty muttered after a few moments, his tone empty. "So am I." He turned away, not quite sure where he intended to go. Backstage, maybe. Zeke Peters would still be there. He'd undoubtedly get a laugh out of this situation.

"Uh, Marty?"

Marty glanced over his shoulder.

"I did see who she left with. Is that any help?"

Marty pivoted around, his body rigid. "Who?"

"Huh?"

"Who did she leave with?"

"Oh. Barry Cooperman. You know, the agent who handles—"

"The woman who was sitting at this table left The Funny Farm with Barry Cooperman?" Marty tried to moderate his tone but couldn't.

The waiter paled beneath his tan and took a step backward. He gulped audibly. "Uh-uh—"

No, Marty told himself fiercely. It couldn't be. She'd been alone at the table. He was positive of it. And the last time he'd seen Cooperman, the agent had been schmoozing and boozing at the bar!

"You saw her leave with him?" he pressed. "You're absolutely sure?"

The waiter bobbed his head. "I, uh, think they went out the back exit."

Marty Knight was not a brawler. He despised violence and those who used it to establish their power over other people. Only once had he surrendered to the atavistic urge to hit another human being. He'd vowed he'd never do it again.

What he saw when he stepped out into the dimly lit, trash-littered parking alley behind The Funny Farm made him forget that vow.

Barry Cooperman was attacking the green-eyed redhead. *His* green-eyed redhead. The agent had her pinned against some kind of low-slung sports car. She was fighting to break free, but the odds were against her. Cooperman topped six feet; she wasn't much more than five-three.

"Barry, stop it!" Marty heard her cry out.

Something inside him snapped. "You son of a bitch!" he yelled, charging across the alley. "Leave her alone!"

Seizing Cooperman with both hands, Marty hauled him off the auburn-haired woman and heaved him aside. The agent stumbled backward several steps then lost his balance. He crashed into a garbage can, knocking it over as he fell to his hands and knees.

Marty pivoted back to the redhead. Her pallor was plain even in the alley's limited illumination. He sensed, rather than actually saw, that she was shaking. He realized he was shaking a little, too.

"Wh-what—?" she stammered, bringing her arms up and crossing them in front of her. The movement made the bracelets on her left arm clink together.

"It's okay," he said quickly. He wanted to caress her cheek or stroke her hair, but he was afraid his uninvited touch might spook her. He pitched his voice to reassure. "It's okay. You're safe. I'm not going to let him hurt—"

Her green-eyed gaze flicked away from his face. Her features went rigid. "Look out!" she gasped.

Marty whirled, narrowly avoiding a clout to the head from Barry Cooperman's right fist.

The agent cursed and grabbed hold of him.

They battled like wrestlers. Grappling. Grunting. Fingers gouging into each other's flesh. Marty knew Cooperman was three or four inches taller and at least forty pounds heavier than him, but he didn't care. He felt a slackness in the other man's body, a slackness some gut-level instinct told him he could turn to his advantage.

He understood the source of that slackness when he caught a whiff of the agent's breath a few seconds later. The smell of whiskey was unmistakable.

Marty almost gagged. His stomach started to churn. His throat tightened and a brackish taste flooded his tongue.

Physical violence . . . and the smell of Scotch.

They made him want to vomit.

Physical violence . . . and the *stench* of Scotch. The stench of unspoken secrets. Of unadmitted shame.

Funny? a voice grated inside his head. *You think I'm funny, you little bastard? Is that what you're laughing at? C'mere, I'll give you funny—*

For one of the few times in his life, Marty Knight didn't see the blow coming.

Two

Three days later, Donna Elizabeth Day sat in her tiny office at the Better Day Center for Children and tried to explain her back-alley encounter with Marty Knight to a colleague.

It wasn't easy. Donna had yet to figure out how to explain the unsettling episode to herself, much less to anyone else. *Especially* not to someone who'd already read a wildly inaccurate account of the incident in a well-known tabloid.

"All right," said the tall, casually dressed woman sitting opposite her. The woman was Dr. Lydia Foster. In addition to being her supervisor at the Center, Lydia was one of the closest friends Donna had ever had. "Let me see if I've got *your* version of the story straight."

"It's not *my* version, Lydia," Donna objected, fiddling with the wide silver and turquoise bracelet that encircled her left wrist. "It's the truth."

"Mmm," the other woman responded neutrally, glancing at the folded newspaper she'd tossed on Donna's cluttered desk about fifteen minutes before. "To review. You agreed to go out with Barry Cooperman as payback for his getting a couple of his clients to attend our next Celebrity Saturday.''

Donna grimaced at her friend's blunt characterization of her date with Barry.

"Don't give me that expression," Lydia chided, wagging a finger. "I wasn't being critical. You're the reason those Saturdays are so successful. If you weren't willing to go all the way—''

"Lydia!"

"What?"

"I do not 'go all the way' to get people to show up for our Celebrity Saturdays.''

"For heaven's sake, I didn't say you did. I said you were *willing* to. A small but significant difference.''

"Oh, right.''

Lydia cocked a brow. "You're not going to deny you'd do almost anything—including peddling your lily white body to the highest bidder—if you thought it would help one of our kids, are you?''

Donna grimaced a second time but decided to hold her tongue. While she knew her friend's question was intended as a joke, it still cut very close to the bone. She *was* prepared to do almost anything to improve the lives of the children at the center. As to where she'd draw the line between "almost" and "absolutely," well, she'd been on the staff at the center for more than five years and she had yet to find out.

Lydia patted her intricately braided hair. "Back to your story," she said in a businesslike manner. "Cooperman took you to dinner at some pretentious restaurant, where he spent most of the meal pitching some script he wants your father to read. Then he dragged you to The Funny Farm.''

"He didn't drag me," Donna disputed. "I don't let anybody drag me anyplace. I like going to The Funny Farm. I wish I had time to stop by more often. It's got some of the best stand-up in L.A. Besides, the owner's an old friend of my father's.''

"Whatever." Lydia brushed these caveats aside. "Cooperman took you there, then dumped you at a table so he could go off and do business at the bar.''

"That's how agents behave, Lydia."

"No, Donna," came the sassy retort. "That's how men whose mamas didn't teach them any manners behave. But you didn't mind, did you? Because while you were sitting at that table all by your lonesome, Marty Knight strutted out on stage and started coming on to you."

Instantly, inevitably, Donna's brain flashed up the compelling image of a dark-haired man with a sensual mouth and vibrantly intelligent brown eyes. She shoved the vivid mental picture away. After three days of practice, she was approaching the point where she could push Marty Knight's face out of her mind before her body started responding to it. Maybe after another three days—three weeks? three months? three years?—she'd be able to do something about getting his face out of her dreams, as well.

Then again, maybe not.

The strange thing was, she'd seen Marty Knight on TV many times. While she'd always found him intriguing, to say nothing of incredibly funny, she'd never been conscious of any real tug of attraction. But now that she'd seen him in the flesh...

"I never said Marty Knight came on to me," she protested, painfully aware that her cheeks were flaming. Although she knew a lot of women envied her translucently fair complexion, she personally cursed its volatility. She'd come of age hoping that her tendency to color up at the slightest provocation would fade with maturity. Unfortunately she blushed as deeply at thirty as she had at three or thirteen.

Lydia made a show of surveying Donna's face. "Honey, you didn't have to," she drawled. "I figured it out for myself. I've got a Ph.D. in psychology, remember?"

"It wasn't like that."

"No? Then what was it like?"

Donna ran her tongue over her lips. "Marty Knight...*looked* at me," she said uncomfortably.

"Uh-huh. And you looked at him."

Donna felt the flush on her cheeks intensify. She shifted involuntarily, remembering the surge of response she'd experienced the first time Marty Knight's gaze had connected with hers at The Funny Farm. She'd blushed, her entire body suffusing with a sweet rush of heat as she'd felt herself embraced without a touch, understood without a word. The intimacy of that initial eye contact had shaken her to the core.

"And he looked some more," her friend went on.

"Lydia, he was on stage doing a set!"

"So?"

"So, it was stand-up, not seduction."

The other woman arched her brows. "Donna, I've seen Marty Knight on TV and I'm willing to bet it's seduction with him whether he's standing up, sitting down or lying flat on his stomach. The man is *hot*. But, to continue . . . Marty Knight finished his act and went offstage. Cooperman came back to the table and said it was time to go. Only one quick whiff of his breath told you he'd been doing more than business at the bar. Naturally, you sweet-talked him into giving you his car keys." She paused a beat then asked, "Right?"

"More or less," Donna affirmed.

"Good. Now, everything seemed pretty cool until you got to the parking alley. That's when Cooperman made a grab for the keys, yes? Then, maybe fifteen seconds later, Marty Knight came out the back door of the club and got the idea Cooperman was making a grab for something a little more personal." Lydia paused again, obviously waiting for Donna's endorsement of her summation.

Donna's gaze flicked from her friend's face to the folded newspaper on the desk. She nodded once, conscious of a curious fluttering in the pit of her stomach.

"One thing led to another and your would-be white knight wound up stretched out on the ground," Lydia continued briskly. "Meantime, your escort for the evening tried to make a quick getaway. Only he was too drunk to drive and he plowed his car into a wall." She made a face. "So there you were, with two unconscious men. One in the gutter with his head in your lap, the other slumped over his steering wheel. And while you were debating what to do, the owner of The Funny Farm, ah, what's his name again?"

"Zeke. Zeke Peters."

"Oh, yes. That's right. And while you were debating what to do, Zeke Peters turned up and took charge. He sent you home in a taxi and hauled the testosterone twosome off to the local emergency room." Lydia eyed Donna expectantly. "End of story?"

Donna swallowed. "End of story."

There was a short silence. Finally, Lydia steepled her fingers together. "I think I like the tabloid's version better."

Donna groaned. She should have known. She really should have.

"I didn't say I *believed* it."

"Well, I should hope not!"

"Come on, Donna. Lighten up. You've got to admit that there's something interesting about the idea of you having a secret affair with Marty Knight."

"Oh, sure," Donna countered, feeling herself start to flush once more and hating it. "It's almost as interesting as the tabloid's contention that I got fed up with his no-strings approach to love and decided to use Barry Cooperman to make him jealous."

"Yeah, well, you probably could have made a better choice than old Barry," Lydia conceded. "Still, he obviously got the job done." She reached forward and picked up the newspaper, displaying its front page with a flourish. "I mean, look at this."

"No, thank you," Donna refused tartly. "I already have."

The "this" to which Lydia had referred was a boldly lettered headline: Knight In Fight For Day's Daughter! Beneath the headline was a photograph of a man and woman locked in what appeared to be a torrid embrace. The darkly attractive man was Marty Knight. The voluptuously shaped woman was . . .

Well, she was—and she wasn't—Donna Elizabeth Day. Mostly, she wasn't.

Donna could live with the cutesy-poo headline, misleading as it was. She could even endure the inaccurate and innuendo-laden article inside the tabloid if she didn't think about it too much. And she certainly didn't intend to think about it at all after this conversation was over.

But that photograph. That damned, doctored photograph! It was so...cheesy. So utterly *sleazy*.... It wasn't even her body. Nonetheless, Donna was willing to bet that the seeing-is-believing public would accept it at face value.

Donna slumped down in her seat, fiddling with her silver and turquoise bracelet once again.

"Now, don't get all bent out of shape, Donna," Lydia advised. "Nobody who knows you is going to take this rag seriously. And as for the folks who don't know you—" The woman shrugged and threw the newspaper onto the desk. It landed front page up.

"Thanks," Donna replied after a moment, wrestling down the urge to turn the tabloid over. She smiled crookedly. "I needed to hear that."

"Then I'm glad I said it," Lydia answered immediately. She waited a beat, then leaned toward Donna, a teasing glint dancing in her dark eyes. "Of course, even your best friend might wonder a little about that picture."

Donna stopped smiling. "That picture is the most blatant composite shot I've ever seen in my life," she stated through gritted teeth. "It's so phony it's almost funny! How anyone could have the unmitigated gall to stick *my* head on some *other* woman's body—"

"Hey, at least it's an attractive body."

Donna made a derisive sound. "It's about six inches taller and two bra sizes bigger than mine."

"More like three."

"Huh?"

"More like three bra sizes bigger. Not that you're flat-chested or anything. But let's get real. Whoever that body belongs to, she's obviously got major-league boobs. I wonder if she's had implants."

"Who knows?" Donna returned with an edge.

"Marty Knight, probably," Lydia answered dryly.

"Who cares?" Without really considering the implications of what she was doing, Donna yanked the tabloid closer to her and began leafing through it.

There were a few moments of silence.

"I take it your father's seen the paper?" Lydia eventually inquired.

Donna paused, her fingers hovering over an item detailing how daily doses of chocolate could enhance a woman's sex drive, then glanced up at her friend. "Excuse me?"

"You were talking to your father on the phone when I came in, right? From what little I heard, I got the impression that your, ah, involvement with Marty Knight was the main topic of discussion."

Donna sighed. "Actually, it was the *only* topic of discussion."

"Donnie's playing the protective papa again?"

"Definitely." Donna smiled ruefully, recalling the conversation. "He may have come to the role later than a lot of fathers, but he's really thrown himself into the part."

"Did you tell him the same story you told me?"

"Pretty much."

"Did he buy it?"

"Mmm . . . pretty much."

"So he's not upset anymore?"

"About the article and the picture, no. But he's still not happy about the headline."

"'Knight In Fight For Day's Daughter'?" Lydia quoted. "What's wrong with that? I mean, considering some of the stuff the tabloids used to write about you . . ." She paused, clearly reluctant to dredge up unpleasant memories.

"I know. I know," Donna murmured, unruffled by her friend's reference to her rocky past. It had taken a lot of time and work, but she'd come to terms with most of the mistakes she'd made while growing up. She'd even come to terms with the fact that she'd made a few of those mistakes in an appalling public manner. "He's upset about the order of the names."

"Say what?"

Donna laughed. "Donald Day doesn't like to take second billing to anyone. Especially to another comic."

"A show biz thing, huh?"

"It usually is with him."

There was another brief silence. Donna continued leafing through the paper, absently noting that the Pentagon allegedly was covering up the fact that an alien from outer space had given birth to twins fathered by Elvis Presley.

"They're all right, aren't they?" Lydia queried finally.
Donna looked up. "Who?"

"Marty Knight and Barry Cooperman. Who else?"

"Oh." Donna looked down again. "Yes. Zeke called me the next morning. They had a few cuts and bruises. Nothing serious."

"That's good."

Donna toyed with the edge of the tabloid page, debating whether to turn it. She knew what she'd see if she did. The question was: Did she *want* to see it?

The answer to that question was yes . . . and no.

"Have you heard from either of them?"

"What?"

"Have. You. Heard. From. Either. Of. Them?" Lydia repeated distinctly.

Donna shook her head, her hair shifting with the movement. "No." Then she realized she wasn't being entirely accurate and she switched to a nod. "Well, actually, yes. In a way . . . sort of. But not directly." She cleared her throat, feeling like an idiot. After a moment, she concluded lamely, "Know what I mean?"

"Honey, I haven't got a clue."

Donna shifted her weight and went back to fiddling with the newspaper. She didn't like the way she was acting. She didn't like it at all. Unfortunately she didn't have any brilliant ideas for modifying her behavior.

"I heard from Barry," she finally admitted. "He sent me a dictated but groveling note of apology and two bottles of champagne."

"*Champagne?*"

"You want it?"

Lydia ignored the offer. "The man actually sent you champagne?"

"Well, I would have preferred flowers or chocolates," Donna conceded lightly. "But it's hardly an indictable offense."

"Doesn't he realize you don't drink?"

"Evidently not."

"You didn't say anything to him?"

Donna shook her head and returned her gaze to the tabloid. While she didn't hide what she was and how it had affected her life, she didn't make a habit of baring her soul to every Tom, Dick or Barry, either.

After a moment, she flipped to the next page in the paper. Braced though she was, she still felt her pulse accelerate.

There was nothing phony or funny about the photograph that confronted her. It was a close-up of Marty Knight's face. He was staring straight into the lens of the camera. The right corner of his long-lipped mouth was starting to curl upward.

The set of his head held a hint of challenge, a hint somehow underscored by the mussed-up state of his thick, dark hair and the slightly crooked line of his nose. His barely begun smile was dangerous. It seemed to promise the kind of "bad" a lot of women considered better than "good." As for the expression in his riveting brown eyes—

Donna glanced away from the picture, acutely aware that her heart was beating much too quickly. She didn't want to see what was in Marty Knight's eyes. She'd seen too much in them already.

"You haven't heard from him, have you?" Lydia asked. There was no need for her to specify who the "him" was.

Donna took a deep breath, then exhaled it very, very slowly. "No," she said, shutting the tabloid with a hand that was less than steady.

"But you'd like to." It wasn't a question.

"Well . . ." It wasn't an answer. But Donna knew no answer was necessary. After a moment, she lifted her gaze to meet Lydia's.

"Two words of advice," her friend declared, then pointed at the telephone sitting on Donna's desk. "Call him."

Donna felt her cheeks go pink. "I can't do that."

"Why not?"

"Because."

"Because why? Because you're the girl and he's the guy and the guy's supposed to make the first move?" Lydia's tone was sardonic. It was the tone of a woman who unabashedly admitted that she'd chased her husband until he'd caught her. "It seems to me Marty Knight's made the first move. The first *couple* of moves, in fact. He probably figures it's your turn."

Donna hesitated for a moment, then said slowly, "I—I'm not sure he's interested."

"You're not sure? Give me a break! You've already admitted the two of you were doing eyeball aerobics while he was on stage at The Funny Farm."

"Yes, but—"

"He also risked life and limb to save you from Cooperman."

"Yes, but—"

"But what?"

Donna was much blunter than she'd intended to be. "Afterward he acted as though he couldn't have cared less," she said flatly.

Lydia looked puzzled. "Afterward when?"

Donna frowned, remembering the moment when Marty had finally responded to her pleas to open his eyes. For a few dizzying seconds, she'd felt as though she'd been peering straight into his soul. He'd been utterly open to her. Completely vulnerable. And then, after catching a glimpse of anger so intense she'd actually flinched from it, Donna had seen his defenses go up. In the space of a few erratic heartbeats, he'd shut her out. His demeanor had become even more aloof once he'd gotten to his feet.

"After he regained consciousness," she told her friend quietly.

"You didn't say anything about this before."

"It didn't seem ... important." That was a lie. Donna knew it. She suspected Lydia knew it, too.

"I see," Lydia responded. She clicked her tongue. "He tried to brush you off?"

"Not tried. Did."

"You offered help, he growled?"

"Several times."

"You told him you appreciated what he'd done, he grunted?"

"Well, actually, the noise he made wasn't as articulate as a grunt."

Lydia cogitated for several seconds, then nodded her head. "Forget what I said about his waiting for you to make the next move," she announced decisively. "The reason you haven't heard from Marty Knight is that he's embarrassed."

"Embarrassed? Embarrassed about what?"

"Messing up his rescue attempt, probably."

"That's ridiculous."

"Maybe. It's also typical male weirdness."

Donna blinked, grappling with this fresh interpretation of Marty Knight's behavior. "Do you honestly believe—?"

"Absolutely."

"But there's no reason for him to be embarrassed!"

"You know that and I know that," Lydia replied crisply. "But Marty Knight apparently doesn't. One of us really ought to tell him, don't you think? And given the fact that I'm a happily married woman with two gorgeous kids, it probably shouldn't be me. Not that I'd mind meeting the man, you understand. I dig his sense of humor. That routine he does about going to parochial school—you know, the one about the nuns so tough they wore black leather habits—cracks me up. He's also got one of the cutest butts I've ever seen . . ."

The hook dangled, baited and ready.

Donna's gaze strayed briefly back to the photograph on the tabloid's front page. Marty Knight did, indeed, do very appealing things for the back of a pair of jeans.

"I don't know his telephone number," she said after a moment, fluffing her hair.

Lydia chuckled. "I'll bet you know somebody who does."

"You don't have to say anything," Marty told the balding, bespectacled man who'd just appeared in the doorway of his dressing room. The man was Arnold Golding, the creator and executive producer of *Murphy's Law*. "I know I stank."

Arnold sneezed. As the victim of multiple allergies, sneezing was something he did very frequently. He was extremely proficient at it.

Arnold pulled an unsanitary-looking handkerchief from his jacket pocket and used it to mop his pinkened nose. "I woubint doe thad faw, Mardy," he responded.

"Well, I would," Marty said, tossing the script he'd been holding aside. He leaned back against the pricey leather couch the decorator who'd done his dressing room two years before described as a "major statement of ambient authority." Refurbishing his dressing room had not been his idea. His agent had insisted on demanding that perk—and a great many others—when his contract had come up for renegotiation at the end of the first season of *Murphy's Law*.

"So your timing—achoo!—was a little off." Arnold sniffled and wiped his nose again. "It was only the first read-through of the week. The script needs a lot of polishing."

"The script wasn't the problem, Arnold. I was." Marty raked his hands through his dark hair. He usually breezed through the show's Monday morning read-throughs. Not today. Today he'd been lead-footed rather than light on his toes, tongue-tied rather than quick with a quip. He'd sat at the rehearsal table and stared down at the script. But instead of focusing on the material, his brain had been fogged by the image of a green-eyed redhead he'd seen from a stage and met in a back alley.

Dammit, he had to get Donna Day out of his head!

"You were distracted," Arnold said mildly, crossing to the couch and plunking himself down. "You want to talk about it?"

"What's to talk about?"

"How about 'Knight In Fight For Day's Daughter'?"

Marty grimaced. "You saw the tabloid, too, huh?"

"One of the guys on the crew showed me."

"Only one? I must have had that damned paper shoved under my nose ten times this morning."

"Yeah, well, it's been a while since you made the front page of that rag. So—achoo!—what's this thing you've got going with Donnie Day's daughter?"

"Nothing."

"Huh?"

"I don't have anything going with her, Arnold. Nada. Zero. Zilch. I barely know the lady."

But, God . . . he'd like to.

Yeah. Sure. Right. He'd also like to sprout wings and fly. And, all things considered, Marty figured his chances of doing that were about as good as his chances of getting to know Donna Day.

"Really?" Arnold persisted.

"Really."

"What about—" a pause for nose-wiping "—your beating the crap out of Barry Cooperman?"

"Reports have been greatly exaggerated."

Arnold heaved a snuffly sigh. "Too bad."

"If you say so."

"Too bad about Donnie Day's daughter, too. She's got an incredible body."

Marty stiffened. Just how did Arnold Golding know about Donna Day's body? he wondered. And where in the hell did he get off making a salacious remark about it?

"What's that supposed to mean, Arnold?" he asked sharply.

The executive producer blinked, a hint of alarm entering his expression. "Hey, hey, take it easy, Marty. I wasn't being personal. I just couldn't help noticing—uh, it's Donna, right? Her name is Donna?"

"Yes."

"Okay. Okay. I just couldn't help noticing Donna's, uh, body in that picture of the two of you."

"Oh, God. That." Marty relaxed a bit. "That's not hers."

"What?"

"The photo's a cut-and-paste job. Donna's face, somebody else's . . . form."

"Oh. Ah, ah, *CHOO!*" Arnold wielded his crumpled handkerchief once again. "You know, I thought there was something strange about the way her head was tilted. So—achoo!—whose is it?"

Marty picked up the script he'd discarded a few minutes before, hoping Arnold would take the hint and leave him alone. "Whose is what?"

"The body. In the picture."

Marty shrugged, genuinely indifferent.

"That *is* you, isn't it?" the executive producer persisted. "On the front page, I mean. Your face. Your... *form?*"

Marty glanced up. "Yeah. Unfortunately."

"You spent time glued up against a body like the one in that photograph and you can't tell me who it belongs to?" Arnold shook his head. "Marty, Marty, Marty. That's not normal."

"Let's just say I don't remember *every* body I run into," Marty answered, shifting his attention back to his script. He turned to the page where John Doe, the unorthodox subpoena server he played on *Murphy's Law,* made his entrance.

There was a short pause. Arnold sneezed twice, then honked into his handkerchief once again.

"Tell me about Donna Day," he suggested softly after several seconds.

Marty's breath seemed to wedge at the top of his throat. He wouldn't have been able to speak even if he'd wanted to, which he didn't. He had no intention of sharing anything about Donna Day with anyone.

He wasn't going to tell Arnold about the way her auburn hair trapped the light and tempted a man's fingers. He wasn't going to describe how the fair, fragile skin of her face seemed to glow from within, either. As for the unexpected flecks of gold in her green eyes...the innate elegance of her posture... the spicy-sweet scent of her perfume...

"She has an amazing laugh," he murmured, scarcely aware that he was speaking aloud. "It reaches right down inside you. It's...I don't know. You have to hear it to understand what I mean. To *feel* it. And when I knew that laugh was mine Friday night...." He clenched his hands, his voice trailing off.

There were a few seconds of total silence.

"You barely know the lady, huh?" Arnold finally asked.

Marty came back to the present with a bump. "I met her once, Arnold," he said stiffly. "One time. That's it."

"But you wouldn't—achoo!—mind meeting her again."

"It's not going to happen."

"Why not?"

Marty hesitated. Then, without equivocation, "Because I made a goddamned jerk out of myself in front of her."

Arnold's eyes widened. "How?"

"You don't want to hear."

"That bad?"

"Worse." There'd been an instant, right after he'd regained consciousness, when he would have sworn he'd died and gone to heaven. To open his eyes and look up into Donna's face had been . . . God! And then, barely a second later, reality had set in and he'd remembered what had happened. His sense of humiliation had been so bitter he'd been able to taste it.

The taste had been all too familiar.

He knew he'd made everything worse by being rude to her. But he hadn't been able to stop himself. He'd learned, very young, to take his lumps alone. To succumb to the lure of another person's compassion—to let down his guard for even a moment—was too dangerous to risk doing.

Arnold wiped his nose. "Women get off on that, you know."

"What?"

"Men making jerks out of themselves," the other man elaborated matter-of-factly. "I think it reinforces their sense of superiority. I mean, deep down they're ninety-nine and nine-tenths percent positive we're idiots. Still, they like to have it confirmed every once in a while."

Marty snorted.

"Hey, I'm serious," Arnold insisted. He paused, eyeing Marty assessingly. "I think you ought to call her."

Marty slapped his script shut. "No."

"Come on. Give yourself a break."

"No!"

Arnold Golding had not become as successful as he was by taking no for an answer. "Okay, then, give *me* a break."

"Give you—what do you have to do with this?"

The executive producer sighed. "I lied to you when I came in here," he declared dolefully. "You *did* stink during the read-through. And I've got this nasty feeling in my stomach—you know, right around the place where people get ulcers—that you're going to go *on* stinking until you get this thing with Donna Day taken care of. I don't like that feeling, Marty. I don't like it at all.''

"Arnold—"

"Call her. Do it for you. Do it for me. Hell, do it for the *laugh.*"

"The laugh?"

"Yeah." Arnold nodded. "The one you said was yours Friday night."

Marty felt his body tighten. He forked his fingers through his hair. "I don't know her telephone number."

Arnold sneezed wetly. "I'll bed you doe sumboddy who duz.''

Three

────

"**S**o you must have phoned Zeke about five minutes before I did," Marty concluded, shutting the door on the passenger's side of his car.

"Sounds like it," Donna agreed, smoothing the skirt of the ecru knit dress she had on. Marty had finally called her and asked her out to dinner. She'd gotten home from work early enough to have time to change her clothes before Marty had picked her up. Or, to be more accurate, to hurriedly paw through every item in her wardrobe before finally settling on an outfit she hoped hit the sartorial mean between making no effort at all and trying too hard.

Marty pocketed his keys. He was dressed very much as he'd been three nights before at The Funny Farm—scuffed cowboy boots, faded jeans, and a slouchy but obviously expensive navy jacket. The main difference was that instead of wearing a white T-shirt he had on a white linen shirt. The top three buttons of the shirt were undone, revealing an inverted triangle of tanned, hair-roughened skin.

"No wonder he laughed when I asked if he knew how I could get in touch with you," he said, shaking his head.

A metallic glint pulled Donna's attention to the base of Marty's throat. There was a narrow gold chain around his neck, she noted with a touch of surprise. Marty Knight hadn't struck her as the jewelry-wearing type.

"Zeke laughed?" she questioned, lifting her gaze back to Marty's face.

"Yeah. But he wouldn't fill me in on what he thought was so funny. He kept saying I'd find out before too long."

"Hmm." They walked toward the entrance of a restaurant named La Cocina de Rosa, Rosa's Kitchen, located about eight blocks from The Funny Farm. "He was growling like a grizzly when I talked to him."

Marty chuckled. "You probably woke him up."

"At one-thirty in the afternoon?"

"Hey, when I was on the road, I never rolled out of bed much before three. Of course, I never rolled into it much before dawn, either. Being involved in stand-up isn't exactly conducive to leading a normal life."

They walked a few seconds in companionable silence.

"You really tried to call me twice, huh?" Marty resumed. Donna had told him that when he'd spoken to her approximately six hours before.

Donna felt a tinge of heat enter her cheeks. Zeke Peters had given her about a half dozen telephone numbers when she'd asked him, rather awkwardly, if he had any idea how she could contact Marty Knight. He'd recommended she use the one he said rang in Marty's dressing room at the studio where *Murphy's Law* was produced. After a bit of hesitation, she'd followed his advice.

"Yes, I really tried to call you twice," she confirmed. "But your line was busy both times."

"Probably because I was trying to call you." Marty had gotten Donna's home and work numbers from Zeke. He'd tried the former first and had been greeted by an answering machine. He'd listened to the recorded message all the way through, conscious that the sound of Donna's voice was doing odd things to his nervous system, then hung up without saying a word. He'd tried her work number several times before finally getting through.

"Better Day Center for Children," Donna had said when she'd picked up the phone.

His mouth had gone dry. His palms had started to sweat. "Donna?" he'd finally asked. He'd been thankful his voice hadn't cracked.

There'd been a quick intake of breath from the other end of the line. Not quite a gasp, but close to it. "Marty?" Donna had responded after a moment. "Marty Knight?"

Her instant recognition of his voice had startled him. He hadn't been able to get a fix on her tone. It had held surprise, obviously. But what kind of surprise? The "I dreamed but never dared hope you'd call" type? Or the "I never thought you'd have the nerve to try to speak to me again" variety?

"Yeah," he'd answered. "It is."

"This is very...strange," she'd responded. She'd laughed a little, the sound unexpectedly shy. Marty had suddenly remembered the way she'd blushed at The Funny Farm and wondered whether she was doing the same thing again. "You calling me, I mean," she'd gone on. "Because...well...actually, I've been trying to call you."

"Marty? Marty?"

Marty blinked, abruptly realizing he'd been zoning out. He also realized they'd reached the restaurant. Smooth, Knight, he told himself derisively, reaching for the door. Truly smooth.

"Sorry," he muttered, pulling the door open.

Unsure of what he was apologizing for, Donna confined herself to a murmured word of thanks for his courtesy and started into the restaurant.

"Donna—" Responding to impulse, Marty reached out and caught her by the arm. The sleeves of her dress were short. Her bare skin was very soft against his fingertips. His muscles clenched on an unbidden flash of speculation about the texture of the skin on the rest of her body.

Donna turned, eyes wide, her pulse scrambling. "Yes?"

Marty withdrew his hand. "What would you have said if you'd been able to complete one of those calls you made to me?"

Donna hesitated, then gave him a slow smile. Her voice, when she finally spoke, was husky. "That's for both of us to wonder about."

La Cocina de Rosa was small in size, but bright and boisterous in spirit. Redolent of the scent of home-style cooking, it had the comfortable feel of a neighborhood hangout.

Donna found herself salivating within seconds of walking in.

"I hope you like this place," Marty said as they settled into the table they'd been shown to.

"I'm sure I will," Donna answered, meaning it. She glanced around, intrigued by how little attention Marty seemed to be attracting. It wasn't that the people present didn't know him. He'd fielded several greetings as they'd made their way to their table. But they'd been offhand greetings, not star-struck salutations. Having grown up with a very public figure for a father, Donna knew the difference between the two.

Over the years she'd heard a lot of Hollywood personalities claim they longed to be treated like "ordinary" people. She'd also seen a lot of those same personalities throw tantrums when they got what they allegedly wanted. She was impressed by the fact that Marty apparently felt no need to impress her with his celebrity status.

She was further impressed by his easy interaction with the waiter who arrived at their table about a minute after they sat down.

"*Buenas noches, amigo,*" the wiry young Latino said as he set down the heavily laden tray he was toting.

"*Buenas noches,*" Marty responded. "Donna, meet Emilio Cisneros. Pre-med, U.C.L.A. His mother's the Rosa in *La Cocina*. Emilio, this is Donna Day. A friend."

"Hello," Donna said.

"Hi," Emilio answered after subjecting her to a brief but intense moment of scrutiny. "Nice to meet you." He quickly distributed napkins, silverware and a pair of menus, then placed a heaping basket of tortilla chips plus bowls of salsa and guacamole in the center of the table. "You want the usual to drink, Marty?"

"Yeah, thanks. Donna?"

"We mix a mean margarita here," Emilio volunteered.

Donna smiled and shook her head. "Mineral water for me."

"Twist of lime?"

"Please."

"Okay. Be right back."

"You're obviously a regular here," Donna commented once Emilio was out of earshot.

"Less regular than I used to be," Marty admitted, glancing around. "I found this place about six years ago. For a while I was coming in at least once a week. Then things...changed."

"Murphy's Law?"

"Yeah. My character turned up in the third episode of the first season. It was supposed to be a one-shot deal. Not much more than a walk-on, really. The description in the script read, 'John Doe is an off-the-wall subpoena server who will do anything to get the job done.' For reasons I still haven't figured out, the studio audience went nuts for the character. So Arnold Golding, the executive producer, told the writers to bring him back the next week. I improvised some stuff during rehearsals and they put it into the show. The response was even stronger. Arnold started talking about making John Doe a recurring role. Then the first episode I'd taped aired and whammo. Breakout time. All of a sudden, I was the flavor of the month."

"At which point you said *hasta la vista* to Rosa's and headed to—" Donna mentioned one of Los Angeles' A-list restaurants.

"I take it you've heard this sort of thing before."

"Once or twice."

"Well, to make a long story short, I eventually got over being a legend in my own mind. I drop by Rosa's two or three times a month now. It'd be more often than that if I hadn't moved to the beach about a year ago." He took a chip from the basket and scooped up a liberal dollop of guacamole, then extended the tidbit toward Donna. "Here. Try this."

After a brief hesitation, Donna leaned forward and took a bite. She thought her lips brushed the tips of Marty's fingers as she did so, but she wasn't certain. The possibility that they might have, triggered a tremor deep within her.

Then she registered the taste of the guacamole. It was utterly delicious. "Mmm," she breathed, savoring the voluptuous blend of avocado, tomato and jalapeño pepper. "Oh, Marty. This is ... mmm ..."

"Good?" Marty suggested, popping the remainder of the chip into his own mouth. His voice was steadier than his pulse. While he'd heard some pretty sexy sounds in his life, few of them had been as provocative as the throaty sigh of appreciation his dinner partner had just given.

"Much better than good," Donna declared. "*Great*. I think you should move back from the beach."

Marty swallowed. "What?"

"If living at the beach is why you don't come here as often as you used to, you should move back." The bowl of fiery-looking salsa beckoned. Donna succumbed to its lure, loading up a chip and ferrying it to her mouth.

"Watch it," Marty warned quickly. "That's very—"

For a second, Donna thought her tongue had been napalmed. She tried to inhale but couldn't. She actually felt sweat break out on her forehead.

"—hot," Marty concluded with a sympathetic wince.

"Just in time, I see," Emilio said simultaneously, swooping down on their table with a pair of ice-filled glasses and a large bottle of imported mineral water.

"Help," Donna croaked, fanning her mouth. A moment later she was gulping water.

"Sorry," Marty apologized.

"For what?" Donna countered, setting down her emptied glass. While her voice wasn't quite back to normal, her eyes were sparkling. "That stuff's wonderful!" She looked at their waiter. "Emilio, your mother's a genius."

"I'll tell her you said so," he responded with a laugh. "Look, if you really like spicy food, she's got an unlisted special tonight—"

"Sold, whatever it is," Donna said immediately, picking up her menu and giving it to the younger man.

"Marty?"

"I'm game." Marty, too, handed over his menu.

"It'll take about thirty minutes."

"Would you bring some more guacamole and salsa?" Donna requested.

"And another bottle of mineral water when you have time," Marty added, refilling her glass.

"I'll be back," Emilio promised.

"I guess I did the right thing when I decided to bring you here," Marty commented after a few moments.

"You had doubts?"

"A few . . . dozen." He felt the muscles of his belly contract as he watched Donna lick a morsel of tortilla from the left corner of her mouth.

She lifted her brows, sensing he was serious. "Really?"

He nodded.

"But why?"

Marty ate a dollop of salsa, chasing it down with a healthy swig of mineral water. "I wasn't sure if this was your kind of place."

Donna tilted her head to one side and studied his face for several seconds. "What other places did you consider?"

He shrugged, then reeled off a list of some of the trendiest restaurants in town.

"Hmm." Donna wasn't certain what to make of Marty's response. She supposed many women would view it as a compliment. But did she want to be categorized as one of those many?

She reached for another tortilla chip. Marty did the same thing.

Their fingers touched, just for an instant.

Brown eyes connected with green ones.

For the space of several thudding heartbeats, everything seemed to stand still.

"Ladies first," Marty said finally, pulling his hand back. His voice was a trifle ragged around the edges.

"No, please," Donna demurred, withdrawing her hand, as well. She could feel the peppery sting of hot blood in her cheeks. "Help yourself."

They each drank some mineral water.

Emilio materialized at their table for the third time. "More salsa, more guacamole," he announced, serving the items as he mentioned them. "And I thought you could use another basket of chips."

He hustled off before either Marty or Donna could say a word.

Brown eyes met green ones once again.

They each took a tortilla chip. His went into the salsa, hers into the guacamole. They ate the chips. They drank some water. Neither of them spoke.

"Can I ask you something personal?" Marty questioned after about thirty seconds of silence.

Donna lifted her brows. "You can always ask. I may not answer."

"Okay," he agreed. "What do you have going with Barry Cooperman?"

The inquiry was so far from what she'd expected that Donna was startled into flippancy. "Aside from my using him to drive you into a jealous rage, you mean?" she parried, referring to the tabloid article about the altercation in The Funny Farm's back alley.

Marty's mouth twisted. "Yeah. Aside from that."

"Well, aside from that, I don't have anything going with Barry Cooperman."

"You went out with him."

"Once. And it wasn't really 'going out.' It was, oh, a kind of quid pro quo."

"His quid, your quo?"

Donna grimaced. "Look. Twice a year, the place I work holds what we call Celebrity Saturday. I've been after a couple of Barry Cooperman's clients to come to one. He promised to deliver them."

"Provided you went out with him."

"He wasn't quite *that* blatant about it."

Marty averted his gaze slightly, drumming his fingers on the table and mulling over what he'd just heard. Eventually, he looked back at Donna. "Did I screw things up for you Friday night?"

Donna nearly choked on a mouthful of salsa. "Wumph—" She swallowed twice. "With Barry?"

The disbelief in her voice was enough to lay to rest any niggling doubts Marty might have had about her feelings toward Barry Cooperman.

"No." He shook his head. "With this—what did you call it? This Celebrity Saturday thing."

It took Donna a few moments to understand what he wanted to know. She was touched by his concern. "You mean, will Barry get his clients to renege?"

"Yeah."

"Oh, I don't think so." She smiled. "Judging by the note of apology and expensive champagne he sent me, Barry's eager to make amends."

"Was your note typed?"

"Don't tell me he sent you one, too!"

"And champagne."

Donna narrowed her eyes. "And just what does Barry want from you?"

"What does any agent want?"

"Blood."

"Cynic," Marty teased.

"Realist," she riposted. "I grew up in Hollywood, you know."

Indeed, Marty did know. Zeke had given him a very sketchy rundown on Donna's background after he'd finished having his head examined, so to speak, at the local emergency room.

"I'm a big fan of your father's," he said sincerely. "I used to watch *The Donnie Day Show* when I was a kid. And I've seen his act in Vegas a bunch of times. He's one of the greats."

"Donnie's a fan of yours, too," Donna replied, thinking back to the conversation she and her father had had earlier in the day. She smiled mischievously. "He says you steal his material."

Marty went rigid. "Excuse me."

"It's a compliment," she hastened to explain. "He only makes that accusation about comics he thinks are very talented."

Marty eased back against his seat. "I see."

"Back to the original question. What do you think Barry wants from you?"

Marty shrugged. "He's got some script he wants me to read." He paused, cocking his head. "What do you think he wants from *you?* Aside from the obvious, I mean."

Donna found herself feeling both flattered and flustered by the very male look in Marty's dark eyes. "I'm afraid my 'obvious' is pretty obscure compared to that woman's on the front page of the tabloid."

"Wha—? Oh. The body."

"A friend's, I take it?" She tried to keep the query light. The identity of the woman was none of her business, of course. Still, she couldn't help wondering . . .

"I assume so."

"Are you saying you don't know whose body it is?"

"Well, I realized it wasn't yours right away. Beyond that . . ."

Donna didn't know what to say to this, so she kept quiet. She spent the next few moments eating tortilla chips and debating how to interpret the first part of Marty's last response.

"Lowering your opinion of me?" Marty inquired.

"What?"

"Don't tell me. It's already so low there isn't much point in bringing it down any further."

While his tone was bantering, Donna thought she heard a hint of uncertainty lurking in it. Her memory flashed back to Lydia Foster's theory about why Marty Knight hadn't called her. "Why should I have a low opinion of you?"

Marty poured himself some more mineral water, then topped off Donna's glass, as well. "Aside from the obvious?"

Donna lifted her napkin and patted it against her lips. "Can I ask *you* something personal, Marty?" she countered, harkening back to the question he'd put to her a few minutes earlier.

"As long as it isn't about what *I* have going with Barry Cooperman."

"Very funny."

"I stole it from your father."

Donna knew a bid to distract when she heard it. Instinct told her the man sitting across the table from her was very, very good at rerouting conversations with a quip. That was fine. She happened to be very, very good at getting conversations back on track.

"When you called me this afternoon and asked me to have dinner with you tonight, I made a joke about your being a fast worker," she reminded him after a tiny pause.

He nodded. "And I said it was more a matter of my being afraid of losing my nerve after spending nearly seventy-two hours working it up."

"What did you mean by that?"

Marty stayed silent for several long moments. Donna could practically hear him running through his repertoire of snappy one-liners.

"That *is* personal," he finally acknowledged.

Donna didn't say anything. After a moment Marty averted his gaze. She heard him exhale heavily. She watched him lift his right hand and touch the gold neck chain he was wearing. She had a feeling he wasn't really aware of what he was doing. Eventually he brought his hand down and turned his eyes back toward hers. There was a hint of challenge in his expression.

"I was afraid to call you because I didn't think you'd want to hear from me," he told her flatly.

"Why would you think that?"

"Why?" Marty gave a humorless laugh. "Because a man who gets knocked out in front of a woman doesn't exactly make a good impression."

"Maybe not," she conceded. "But a man who tries to help a woman in trouble certainly does."

"Oh, yeah. Some help I gave you on Friday night, Donna. I came charging to your rescue and ended up flat on my face in the gutter with *you* trying to take care of *me*. Then afterward—God!—I behaved like a total jerk when I came to." Marty grimaced. "If I were you, I wouldn't want to have anything to do with me."

"Well, you're *not* me."

Marty stayed silent for several seconds, apparently mulling this over. "Did you expect me to call?" he eventually asked.

"I don't know if expect is the right word," Donna replied after a moment, feeling her cheeks grow warm once again. "I . . . hoped. But I was afraid you weren't interested."

Marty's brows shot up. "You were what?"

"Well, the way you acted in the alley—"

"What about the way I acted in the club? My God, Donna, I did half my routine staring right at you."

"I didn't say what I felt was logical," Donna returned with a trace of asperity. "You asked me whether I expected to hear from you and I told you."

There was a brief silence.

"I'm sorry," Marty finally said. "I just figured I'd been very . . . obvious." He picked up a chip and dragged it back and forth across the top of the guacamole. Then, "What changed your mind?"

"About what?"

"About my being interested in you. I mean, if you decided to try to call me after nearly three days . . ." He gestured, letting his voice trail off.

"Well, actually, it was someone, not something," Donna admitted after a moment. "A friend of mine saw the tabloid article and picture and wanted to know the real story. One thing led to another and I ended up saying I wasn't sure you were interested in me."

"Because of the way I'd acted in the alley."

"And because you hadn't gotten in touch with me. Anyway, Lydia—that's my friend's name, Lydia Foster—suggested I was reading the situation wrong. She thought that you were interested. She also thought that you were . . . embarrassed . . . by what had happened."

"Lydia Foster sounds like a very perceptive lady."

"Oh, she is. She's a child psychologist."

"Which, of course, makes her eminently qualified to assess the juvenile workings of my mind." The comment was utterly deadpan.

"Oh, Marty, I wasn't implying—"

Marty interrupted her with an easy laugh. "It's okay, Donna. No offense taken. I've had my emotional maturity impugned plenty of times before."

Donna had to smile. "I wasn't impugning, either."

"I guess that will have to wait till you know me better."

The comment was casual, yet it sent a quicksilver tingle of anticipation dancing up Donna's spine. She lowered her lashes, conscious of a sudden acceleration in her pulse rate.

"Do you work with this Lydia Foster?" Marty asked curiously.

Donna looked up. She nodded. "At the Better Day Center for Children."

"Are you the 'Better' Day?"

"Hardly."

"What is the Center? A school?" There was genuine interest in his voice.

"It's a privately funded shelter. Our kids are from severely dysfunctional families. Addicted parents. Abusive parents. You name it. The adults who are supposed to be taking care of these kids can't...or won't. The Center's designed to be a safety net. Unfortunately, for every one child we catch there are dozens we miss because we don't have the space or the staff."

"Yeah, I can imagine," Marty said quietly. There was an expression—part bleak, part brooding, part something Donna couldn't interpret—in his dark eyes. "So you're, what? A social worker? A psychologist?"

"I've got a degree in child psych. I do counseling. Plus a lot of paperwork. And I raise money. Because of who my father is, I've got access to some people with deep pockets. I haven't been shy about hitting them up for contributions."

"What about those Celebrity Saturday things you mentioned earlier? Where do they fit in with what you do?"

"Actually, they got started almost by chance. An old friend of Donnie's said he wanted to visit the Center before he made a donation. So, I arranged to take him on an informal tour one Saturday. The kids all recognized him, of course. They were thrilled with the idea that he'd come to see them. He was absolutely terrific—ended up staying for hours. A week or so later he called and asked if he could visit again and bring a few friends. His friends included several members of the Laker's basketball team. One thing led to another and the end result was our Celebrity Saturdays. They're good for boosting public awareness of the problems the Center deals with. They're also good for boosting contributions. But, most of all, they're good for boosting the kids' self-esteem.''

''And you're in charge of them.''

''More or less. The next one's this weekend, as a matter of fact.''

''Your work at the Center must keep you very busy.''

''It's the most important thing in my life,'' Donna told him frankly. ''Still, I'd give anything to be out of a job.''

Marty frowned. ''I don't understand.''

''I'd love to live in a world where there wasn't any need for places like the Better Day Center for Children.''

Marty stayed silent for what seemed like a long time. Then he said quietly, ''Amen to that.''

Four

Rosa's unlisted special turned out to be *carne adovada,* an entrée that featured chunks of pork marinated to fall-apart tenderness in an incendiary chili sauce.

"Stop me before I eat again," Donna groaned about forty minutes after Emilio had served their main course. She set her knife and fork down on the edge of her dinner plate and pushed the plate away. The movement made the collection of gold and tortoiseshell bangles she was wearing clink together.

"There's more *posole* left," Marty observed, indicating the bowl of lime-soaked hominy corn sitting to his left.

Donna declined with a resolute shake of her head. The gold hoops that dangled from her earlobes swung back and forth against her cheeks.

"Well then, how about having the last *sopaipilla?*" Marty nodded toward the wicker basket placed to his right.

As stuffed as she was, Donna still found herself tempted by the notion of indulging in just one more of Rosa's ethereally delicious puffs of fried bread. Her mouth started to water. She could imagine the taste and texture of the fragile pastry melting on her tongue.

No, she told herself firmly. You've had enough.

She shook her head again.

Marty chuckled. "You'd be a lot more convincing if you weren't drooling, you know."

Donna decided this twitting remark did not deserve to be dignified by a response. She did, however, pick up her napkin and dab at her mouth.

"I could save you from yourself," Marty went on in a reflective tone.

"Oh, really?"

"Uh-huh. I could force myself to eat the last *sopaipilla*."

"Such nobility."

"Hey, what can I tell you? I'm a noble Knight." Grinning, Marty picked up the remaining *sopaipilla* and split it in two. He extended one half toward Donna. "Let's share."

After a tiny pause, Donna leaned forward and accepted the delectable morsel much as she had when he'd offered her the tortilla chip and guacamole at the start of the meal. The difference was that this time she didn't have any doubts about whether or not her lips touched his fingers. She *knew*.

She saw something spark deep in Marty's whiskey-brown eyes.

She felt her heart stutter, then completely skip a beat. She found she had to struggle to swallow the pastry in her mouth.

Her dinner companion, she noted, seemed to have a bit of difficulty getting his half of the *sopaipilla* down, too.

"So—" Donna cleared her throat "—you said something earlier about *Murphy's Law* being just about wrapped for the season?"

One corner of Marty's mouth kicked up. His expression told her he knew exactly what she was trying to do and why she was trying to do it. His expression also told her he was going to let her get away with it . . . this time.

"That's right," he affirmed. "We've got three more episodes to tape, including the big cliff-hanger."

"And you're not doing a movie during hiatus?"

"Not this year. I made a theatrical release last summer and a pair of made-for-TV flicks the summer before that.

Now I want to take a breather. I've got a two-week gig in Las Vegas in June, but that's basically it. I plan to spend July and August lounging around my house."

"Sounds relaxing."

Marty seemed to hesitate. Then, very casually, he remarked, "Maybe you'd like to spend some time doing the same thing."

"What?" Donna toyed with a lock of her hair. Her pulse had speeded up. "Lounging?"

A nod. Still very casual.

"Around your house at the beach?"

Another nod. Not quite as casual as the one before it.

"With . . . you?"

A third and apparently final nod. This one wasn't casual at all.

Donna knew she was beginning to blush. She also knew she didn't care. "Maybe I'd like that very much."

They left La Cocina de Rosa a short while later. While their conversation had shifted back to a bantering mode by that time, Donna was acutely conscious of the sexual tension shimmering beneath their teasing give-and-take.

The drive to her Hollywood Hills home was laced with laughter. Somehow they got caught up in an offbeat word game that involved pairing film titles to create unlikely—and irreverent—double features.

"All right," she said as Marty turned onto the street where she lived. *"Jaws."*

Marty frowned thoughtfully, his eyes on the road. *"Jaws,"* he murmured. "Now let me—" He broke off suddenly, his lips curving into a wickedly triumphant grin. *"A Farewell to Arms."*

"Ugh! Marty, that's sick!"

Marty pulled up in front of her house and braked. "No sicker than your idea of putting *The Deer Hunter* on the same movie bill as *Bambi*," he retorted, turning off the car's engine.

Donna choked back a laugh. "Well . . ."

Marty winked, undid his seat belt and got out.

Donna unbuckled her own seat belt as she watched him walk around to her side of the car. His lean-hipped, long-legged stride was swift and strong. He moved with the grace-sheathed power of a jungle cat.

Something inside her fluttered as her mind flashed back to the almost feral way Marty had taken on Barry Cooperman. The single-mindedness of his attack had frightened her more than the agent's drunken fumbling. But even more terrifying than that had been the way he'd abruptly stopped fighting and left himself utterly vulnerable to his opponent's flailing—

"Donna?"

The sound of her name, spoken low and with a hint of concern, brought Donna back to the present. Blinking, she realized that Marty had opened the door on the passenger side of the car.

"Sorry," she apologized quickly.

"No problem."

Donna swung her legs to the right and got out of the car, smoothing the skirt of her knit dress as she stood up. Marty slammed the car door shut. His body brushed against hers for just an instant. A small tremor of reaction ran through her. She caught her breath. She swore she heard him do the same.

"Are you all right?" Marty's question was quick, quiet, and just a tad too controlled.

Donna lifted her chin slightly. "Just fine."

"Good."

They walked from his car to the front door of her modest, cottage-style house in silence. It was a flawless May night. The moon that hung against the cloudless midnight sky shone like a newly minted silver dollar.

"So," Marty said when they reached their destination.

"So...what?"

"So...I wish I could think of something clever to say."

A breeze sent a lock of hair fluttering across her face. Donna brushed it back into place. "Well, I'm glad you can't."

"You are?"

"Mmm-hmm. It saves me having to think of something clever to say in return."

"Ah."

There was a short silence. Marty turned his head slightly. The chain he wore around his neck glinted in the moonlight.

"What's that?" Donna asked impulsively.

He turned his head back toward her. "What's what?"

"The chain." She wanted to touch it, but pointed instead. "Around your neck."

Marty lifted his hand to the base of his throat, much as he had during dinner. Once again, Donna had the impression that he wasn't entirely aware of what he was doing.

"Oh. This." An odd expression flickered across his mobile face as he spoke. After a moment, he pulled the chain out of his shirt. There was a small religious medal dangling from it. He cupped the medal in his palm. "It was a present."

"From your parents?" Donna guessed. The medal had the time-worn look of a family keepsake.

Marty's fingers closed protectively around the small piece of engraved metal. "No," he said shortly, shaking his head. "From a teacher. Sister Mary Pauline."

Donna let a few moments slip by. She knew she'd blundered, but she didn't know how. Had she made a mistake by referring to his parents? she asked herself. Marty had mentioned during dinner that his father was dead and his mother remarried. She hadn't gotten the impression that he minded talking about them. Of course, she hadn't gotten the impression that they were his favorite topic of conversation, either. But still . . .

"You really did go to parochial school, then?" she finally asked, striving to keep her tone light. "You didn't just make up that routine you do about the ninja nuns in black leather?"

Marty tucked the medal back into his shirt. "Nobody could just 'make up' Sister Mary Pauline," he replied flatly. Too flatly, Donna thought, remembering the way his fingers had fisted around the medal. It took a lot of effort to sound that detached. "But yeah. I really went to parochial school. St. Cecilia's in Chicago. My parents decided the discipline would do me good."

There was something odd about the last sentence, but Donna couldn't quite put her finger on what it was. Maybe it was the way he'd inflected the word "discipline."

"And did it?" she queried. "Do you good, I mean."

He shrugged. "What do you think?" Marty's inquiry was soft, yet there was an edge to it. An edge obviously meant to cut. The question was: To cut whom?

Was he asking for reassurance? Donna wondered. Or was it something more complicated than that? Several times during the evening Marty had deliberately—though very drolly—put himself down. And each time he'd done so, he'd offered her the opportunity to join in his belittlement. Was it rejection he was seeking from her, then? Was it rejection he *expected*?

"Well, I don't know what parochial school did for you," she declared quietly. "But I have a hunch that whatever you got from Sister Mary Pauline—besides the medal—made a big difference in your life."

Marty stiffened, then went absolutely still. He didn't move, didn't speak, didn't seem to *breathe* for close to a minute. Finally he nodded. "Yeah," he concurred. "Sister Mary Pauline was something else."

"Was?"

He didn't really need to respond. The answer was in his eyes. "She died about four years ago."

"Oh, Marty, I'm sorry."

Donna genuinely expected him to turn away. But to her astonishment, he reached out and brushed the knuckles of his right hand gently against her cheek. As light as it was, she felt the contact clear down to her toes.

"Me, too," he told her with devastating simplicity.

Donna remained silent. Deep inside, she was trembling.

"It took me a long time to accept the news," Marty went on, bringing his hand back down to his side. The words came out slowly. Almost reluctantly. Donna had the feeling he was going to tell her something he'd never told anyone else. It was obvious the act of telling didn't come easy to him. "I always figured it'd take a squadron of B-52s to knock Sister Mary Pauline out."

"She was tough, hmm?"

"The toughest." There was both admiration and affection in his use of the superlative.

"'Den Mother to a Hell's Angels gang'?" Donna borrowed a line from one of Marty's best-known routines.

"Have some respect. That's Den Mother *Superior.*"

"Oh. Of course. And what's that tattoo you claim she had?"

Marty smiled briefly. "You mean, Born to Raise Lazarus?"

"Right." Donna wondered how much further she dared probe. "Did Sister Mary Pauline realize she was the inspiration for one of your routines?"

Marty seemed surprised by the question. "Oh, sure."

"She saw you do it?"

"Well, actually, she caught me trying out an early version in the school cafeteria."

"Really?"

"Uh-huh." He smiled again. "She made me write 'I will not take the Lord's name in vain' a thousand times and told me to work on my delivery."

"No!"

"Hey, Sister was right. My delivery was lousy."

"And after that?"

Marty shrugged nonchalantly. "I took her advice and my delivery improved."

For a moment Donna thought he was deliberately trying to deflect her line of inquiry. Then something, some instinct, told her this wasn't the case. Marty had made the quip reflexively.

"No." She shook her head. "What I meant was, did Sister Mary Pauline see you perform after you turned professional?"

Marty didn't answer immediately. A faraway look came into his eyes. Donna had the feeling he was reliving a moment that had meant a great deal to him.

"Yeah," he said finally. "Once. About six months before she died. It was at a club in Chicago. I didn't even know she was in the audience until she came marching backstage after my final set.''

''Marching?''

''She wasn't the type to tiptoe. Especially not when she was in uniform.''

''You mean she came backstage wearing her habit?''

''Nun clothes, head to toe.'' He frowned briefly. ''No. Wait a minute. Make that head to ankle. She was wearing black Reeboks.''

Donna found herself wishing she could have had a chance to meet Sister Mary Pauline. ''She must have made quite an impression.''

Marty chuckled. ''Oh, yeah. And she did a couple, too.''

''I beg your pardon?''

''Sister Mary Pauline did impressions. Mae West. Jimmy Cagney. She wasn't bad. As a matter of fact, her John Wayne was pretty damned good.''

Donna began to laugh. ''John Wayne?''

''You have a problem with the idea of a five-foot-nothing nun pretending to be the Duke?''

''N-no,'' Donna gasped, unable to stem the hilarity bubbling out of her. The image Marty's words conjured up was irresistibly funny. ''Of, of c-course not.''

She was never able to estimate how long she would have gone on laughing if she hadn't registered the sudden change in Marty's face. She couldn't put a name to the expression that transformed his lean features, but she knew she'd seen it once before. She'd seen it during the dizzying seconds when they'd first made eye contact at The Funny Farm.

Humor gave way to something heart-stopping.

Marty lifted his right hand and traced the curve of Donna's cheek with a feathering stroke. She felt herself flush from breast to brow. The faintly callused tips of his fingers drifted downward. Slowly. Oh, so slowly. It was as if he was trying to catalogue every pore on her face.

''Do you have any idea what your laugh does to me?'' he asked. His tone was even more caressing than his touch.

''My l-laugh?'' Donna echoed unsteadily.

Marty nodded, buffing the delicate line of her jaw with the pad of his thumb. "That's the reason I had to find you Friday night."

"I don't—" she swallowed "—understand."

"I heard you laughing while I was sitting at the bar waiting to go on. I couldn't see you—just hear you. And it was...beautiful. The only problem was, you were laughing for somebody else." He brought his left hand up. He cupped her face with both palms and gazed deep into her eyes. "I wanted you to laugh for me, Donna."

Donna realized she'd lifted her own hands and placed them against Marty's chest. She wasn't trying to push him away. She was, in fact, very close to clinging to him.

"You got what you wanted, Marty," she whispered, sliding her palms upward. She experienced a very feminine thrill as she felt his body respond to her touch. "I laughed for you."

"I know you did," he acknowledged huskily. Only a few inches separated them. "The problem is, it wasn't enough."

And then Marty bent his head and kissed her.

Donna melted against him, her breath escaping in a languorous sigh. She yielded to the coaxing play of his lips. He teased her. Tempted her. Taught her a wholly unexpected lesson about her capacity for physical response.

The taste of him emboldened her. She touched his tongue with the tip of her own for a heady half second.

A shy retreat.

A sinuous return.

She heard Marty groan deep in his throat. She felt the sensual tightening of his body. A seductive heat seemed to invade her body at the same time. Her bones turned to liquid.

"Donna..."

"Yes."

She heard the words quite clearly. She simply wasn't certain they'd been spoken aloud.

Her arms were around Marty's neck now. She had no memory of having moved them there. But the when or the why didn't seem to matter. Only the rightness of what was happening was important.

Stretching up on her tiptoe, Donna twined her fingers hungrily into Marty's dark, thick hair. She sensed him shifting his weight, adjusting the fit of their bodies. The intimacy of their embrace increased tenfold.

His tongue moved over hers, claiming the sweetness of her mouth in a gliding, rough velvet stroke. His fingers from one hand were tangled possessively within the silken strands of Donna's hair. The other hand slid down the line of her spine.

Marty nipped at her lower lip, seeming to savor its satiny resilience. A moment later he licked the same bit of flesh. Donna's breath shattered at the top of her throat.

She was shivering like a fever victim when the kiss finally came to an end. She took a step backward and nearly toppled over. Marty caught her, steadied her, then carefully let her go.

After a moment *he* took a step backward.

Donna had no idea how long they stood there, staring at each other. It could have been a few seconds. It could have been a few hours. It could have been some strange combination of the two. The supposedly immutable laws of time and space no longer seemed to apply.

She lifted her hand and touched her mouth. Her fingers were trembling. Her lips felt warm and tender, like sun-ripened fruit.

She knew what she wanted and the knowledge stunned her. She'd only met this man three days ago!

She thought later that she might have whispered Marty's name. She saw him stiffen suddenly and thrust his hands deep into the pockets of his jacket. His lean features hardened, his tanned skin pulling tightly over the strong bones beneath. He drew a shuddery breath as if he was preparing to speak.

Donna waited . . .

The only thing Marty said before he left her was goodnight.

Five

The name on the file Donna was reviewing was Collins, Samuel Mark.

Sam Collins was ten years old and an only child. His mother was dead. His father, Mark, was currently serving a jail sentence for drunken driving. Sam had been removed from his father's custody three months before, after a teacher had reported her belief that he was being abused and a doctor had found physical evidence to support her suspicions.

Donna glanced at the small color photograph that accompanied Sam Collins's file. It showed an unsmiling youngster with buzz-cut hair and belligerent brown eyes.

The eyes hooked her. There was so much anger in them. Far too much for a child. Yet lurking underneath the anger there was vulnerability. It was as though—

Donna stiffened suddenly, an unnerving tingle of recognition skittering up her spine. She'd seen the same kind of vulnerability, the same kind of anger, four days ago. But those brown eyes had belonged to a grown man, not a little boy.

"Donna?"

Donna blinked, her heart performing a hop, skip, and jump. After a moment, she looked across her desk at Lydia Foster. "Yes?"

"Are you okay?"

"Yes," Donna said, nodding quickly. "I just had—" she paused for a split second, then repeated "—yes. I'm fine."

"Mmm." The other woman did not sound convinced.

Donna returned her gaze to Sam's file. She could feel Lydia watching her. The connection she'd just made was a disquieting one for a great many reasons. Of course, making the connection didn't mean it was so. But still . . .

She forced herself to focus on the troubled child at hand. The amount of mental energy it required was distressing to her. She was not accustomed to being distracted from her work by anything.

Turning to the second page of the file, Donna skimmed the first few paragraphs, then came to a stop. Frowning, she reread the salient sentences.

"He ran away from his foster home to break his father out of jail?" she asked disbelievingly, glancing at Lydia once again.

The other woman nodded, her expression grim. "According to Sam, Mark Collins was framed. He also claims the man is the greatest guy on earth."

"Denial."

"All the way," Lydia concurred flatly. "The doctor who examined Sam said he had a plausible story for every cut and bruise on his body. And not one of those stories had anything to do with his father getting drunk and knocking him around."

Donna didn't comment. She'd witnessed the syndrome Lydia was describing more times than she wanted to think about since she'd come to work at the Center.

"So the—" she consulted the file to make certain of the name "—Silenskys are cutting him loose?"

"They're good people, Donna," Lydia emphasized. "But they've got two other foster kids. Sam's just too much for them to handle right now. He's one tough case."

Donna studied the photograph of Sam Collins again. There were a great many adjectives besides tough that could be applied to the youngster who glared up at her. Neither "cute" nor "cuddly" was among them.

But those eyes. Sweet heaven, what she saw in those brown eyes!

"I'd say he's one scared little boy, Lydia." Donna fingered the edge of Sam's file. "I've got a counseling slot open."

Lydia sighed and rose to her feet. "No, you don't. But neither does anyone else. So, Sam Collins is yours until further notice."

"I'll do my best."

"You always do." Lydia got halfway to the door then pivoted back. "Oh. Since you obviously aren't going to volunteer any juicy details, I guess I'll have to ask. Just how did things go with Marty Knight?"

Donna felt her cheeks grow warm. She had to restrain herself from raising her hand and touching her lips. After a few seconds, she offered her friend the answer she'd arrived at after a restless night of contemplating the same question. "To tell the truth," she said slowly, "I'm not sure."

Lydia's brows went up. "You're not—"

Donna's phone rang. She picked it up. "Better Day Center for Children."

"Donna?"

A quiver ran through her. There was no mistaking the identity of the caller.

"Marty?"

"Yeah." The sound of a throat being cleared came through the line. "Look, if you're free tonight, I'd like to see you again. I think we need to talk."

"Ah-choo!"

Startled, Marty nearly dropped the cordless telephone he was holding. He pivoted to confront Arnold Golding, who was standing in the doorway of his dressing room.

The door had been closed. While Marty wasn't certain about a lot at the moment, he was certain about that.

"I knocked a whole bunch of times," Arnold explained nasally. "But you didn't answer. I got worried, Marty."

"Dammit, Arnold—"

"I just wanted to let you know you didn't stink at rehearsal today," the executive producer cut in, mopping his nose with a wad of tissues. "I guess things must have gone pretty well with Donnie Day's daughter, huh?"

Marty's response to this basically rhetorical inquiry was forestalled by the shrilling of his cordless phone. He switched the device on and jammed it against his ear. "What?" he demanded.

"Touchy, touchy, kid," a familiar voice growled.

Marty closed his eyes. "Zeke?"

"Nah. It's your personal version of Directory Assistance. So, Marty. Tell me. Did you and Donna ever connect?"

Talk.

That's what Marty had said he wanted to do. And that's what he and Donna did. They talked, over another delicious dinner at La Cocina de Rosa.

They talked about her work at the Better Day Center for Children and about his work on *Murphy's Law*. They talked about movies, music and Mexican cooking. About smog, sports and scandal. They even talked about the upcoming presidential election.

At the end of an hour and a half, it seemed to Donna that she and Marty had talked about every subject under the sun except the one she was positive was foremost in both their minds. And then, rather than talk about that one crucial subject, they'd lapsed into silence.

Donna would have liked to have blamed the silence entirely on Marty, but she knew she couldn't. She was as responsible for it as he was. She was equally responsible for the impersonal chitchat that had gone before.

This isn't working, she thought.

She chased a bite of Rosa's superb *chilis rellenos* around and around on her plate. She was careful not to let her gaze stray across the table to Marty. Their eyes had caught and clung several times during the meal. On each occasion, she'd had the dizzying sense that the air in the restaurant had gotten very thin.

There'd been silences the evening before, of course. Some of them long and lingering. Some of them short and sharp. And more than a few of them unsettling. But *this* silence—

"This isn't working," Marty announced abruptly.

Donna dropped her fork, stunned to hear the words she'd thought just seconds before coming out of Marty's mouth. The utensil bounced off the table and fell to the floor with a metallic clatter.

"What isn't working?" she asked after a moment.

Marty crumpled his napkin and tossed it down next to his plate. "This waltzing on eggshells we've been doing for the past ninety minutes."

Donna knew she should welcome his directness. Instead her impulse was to back away from it. "Is that what we've been doing?"

"You have another name for it?"

"How about—" she gestured "—making polite conversation?"

"Polite is for people who don't know each other."

There was no way Donna could evade the sledgehammer impact of this last remark. "We only met four days ago, Marty," she pointed out tautly.

"Yeah, well, maybe that's all it takes."

"For what?"

"For whatever the hell's happening between us."

Marty's words jolted Donna's rapidly accelerating pulse like a series of speed bumps. It was several seconds before she trusted herself to speak. "You don't . . . like it?"

"Do you?"

Shaken, she found herself driven to say something she hadn't said since she was a little girl. "I asked you first."

For a moment, Marty seemed on the verge of anger. Then, astonishingly, one corner of his mouth started to curl upward. "So?" he retorted. "I asked you second."

His response captured the nyah-nyah-nyah inflection of childhood perfectly. A sudden bubble of laughter tickled the back of Donna's throat.

"I'll tell you if you tell me," she bargained.

Marty shook his head. "Ladies before gentlemen."

"Age before beauty."

"Pearls before swine."

Feeling slightly giddy, Donna scrambled for an appropriate comeback. She wound up blurting out the first thing that popped into her head. "I before E except after C."

There was a pause.

"Excuse me?" Marty queried with exaggerated courtesy.

Donna flushed. "It was either that or death before dishonor."

"Ah. Tough choice."

There was another pause. It lasted a lot longer than the previous one. Donna spent most of it gazing down at the table.

Finally she forced herself to raise her eyes. All right. No more waltzing on eggshells. "We were talking about what's happening between us," she reminded quietly.

Marty regarded her through narrowed eyes for several seconds. "Yeah," he concurred. "We were." He waited a second or two more, then leaned forward. "Okay. Look. We both know things got . . . pretty heavy . . . last night."

Donna felt a wave of hot blood surge up into her face. The kiss, she thought. He's talking about the kiss.

A tremor ran through her body. She closed her eyes, shifting involuntarily in her seat.

Donna Day had never experienced anything like the kiss she'd shared with Marty Knight less than twenty-four hours earlier. She'd never experienced anything like her explosively uninhibited response to it, either.

At least, not that she could remember.

Something painful stirred to life deep within her. It was an emotion she'd thought she'd put behind her many years ago. The emotion was shame.

"I'm not like that," Donna asserted fiercely, opening her eyes.

Marty stared at her. "What?"

"I'm not like that," she repeated, clenching her hands. "The way I was when you kissed me. The way I acted. I'm not like that."

"I never thought—"

"I'm not easy, Marty," she insisted. "I'm not."

"Don't you think I know that?" he asked, an edge of anger entering his voice. "One of the reasons I stopped when I did was that—"

"You just walked away," she interrupted, her jumbled feelings boiling over. "One moment you were kissing me, the next moment you were—"

"Dammit, Donna, I was scared!"

That stopped her cold. "S-scared?" she finally stammered.

"Yeah." Marty nodded. *"Scared.* Things were happening too fast and it scared the hell out of me."

"But—"

"I don't like losing control. And that's what I was on the edge of doing last night. Hearing you laugh. Touching you. Kissing you..."

His voice frayed into an electric silence.

"I'm not going to pretend I haven't gone the hit-and-run route when it comes to sex," he went on after a few moments. His tone was flat. Donna could see the effort it cost him to keep it that way. "I spent a lot of years on the comedy circuit, and I didn't spend them like a monk. I did some things—some stupid, selfish things—before I finally grew up."

Marty paused, clearly struggling with what he was going to say next. Finally he concluded, "But that was then and this is now. That was other women and this is...this is you, Donna. This is *us.* And it feels different. I don't know how or why, but it does. And I don't want to mess it up."

Donna swallowed hard. Her heart was racing. After a few breathless seconds, she matched his admission with her own. She had no other choice. "I don't want to mess it up, either, Marty."

Emotion blazed in his brown eyes. "Are you sure?"

She nodded.

With great deliberation, Marty reached across the table and clasped Donna's hands with his own. "Then let's back up," he urged. "I don't mean we should pretend what's happened hasn't happened. But maybe...maybe we can take whatever it is we've got going a little slower."

A tinge of color stole into Donna's cheeks. "Maybe we can take it a *lot* slower."

A moment later she let her fingers intertwine with his.

"What are you doing this weekend?" Donna asked, pausing in the act of unlocking her car door. She and Marty had driven to La Cocina de Rosa separately. He'd insisted on escorting her to where she'd parked.

Marty raised his brows. "This is your idea of taking things slowly?"

"I didn't mean it *that* way, Marty."

"No? Exactly what way did you mean it, then?"

"I was wondering if you'd like to come to Celebrity Saturday at the Center. I don't know if you remember me telling you, but it's this weekend."

Marty remembered, all right. He remembered everything Donna had said to him. "Me?" he echoed uncomfortably. He hadn't foreseen this. He realized he should have.

She nodded, her mouth curving into a lovely smile. "You'd be great."

Marty shifted his weight from one foot to the other. He forked a hand back through his hair. "Uh, what would you expect me to do?"

Donna's smile contracted. It was obvious she was surprised by his question. "Do?" she repeated quizzically. "Well, um, basically, I'd expect you to show up and be yourself."

"Easier said than done," he quipped quickly. "Couldn't I be somebody else? Like, oh, one of the Teenage Mutant Ninja Turtles, maybe?"

"Actually, the Turtles are already on the guest list."

"Oh, really?" Marty was stalling and he knew it. He also knew he wasn't doing a very subtle job of it.

"Really," came the quiet affirmation. Donna's smile had disappeared completely. An odd expression had come into her eyes. She made a small gesture. "Look, Marty, it was just a thought. You've probably got a million things planned for this Saturday. I know how busy you are."

Busy had nothing to do with his reluctance to accept her invitation. But he couldn't tell her that. Telling her that would require too many explanations. Explanations he wasn't ready to offer to anyone, let alone her.

"Kids from severely dysfunctional families," she'd said when she'd described the youngsters the Center tried to help. Kids with addicted parents. Abusive parents. Kids with parents who couldn't—or wouldn't—take care of them.

Marty didn't know if he'd be able to handle it.

"I'm not very good with kids," he said after a few seconds. He wondered if the excuse sounded as lame to her ears as it did to his.

Donna tilted her head to one side, her auburn hair shifting around her heart-shaped face. "I think you may be underestimating yourself," she returned. "Some of the kids at the Center are big fans of yours."

Instinct made him reach for a joke. "Only *some* of the kids?"

"*Murphy's Law* comes on too late for the little ones."

"You could always tape it for them."

"Well, yes," she agreed wryly. "We could always do that." She paused, studying his face silently. Marty felt his body start to tighten. After several seconds Donna resumed speaking. "But…anyway. As I said, I realize how busy you are. I don't want you to think I'm trying to pressure—"

"I'll come," he interrupted, unable to stand the disappointment in her voice.

Donna blinked. "What?"

"I'll come to Celebrity Saturday."

"You will?"

He nodded once, not trusting himself to say more.

She gave him a smile as warm as summer sunshine. "That's wonderful!"

"Yeah, well…" Her pleasure at his announcement made Marty feel like the worst kind of hypocrite.

"The program starts at noon and runs until five," Donna informed him. "Drop by anytime. It's very casual. There'll be food. Hamburgers, hot dogs, that sort of thing. Plus giveaways for the kids."

Marty latched onto the giveaway idea as if it were a lifeline. Yeah, he thought. Giveaways sounded good. It would

definitely take the edge off if he showed up at the Center
bearing gifts.

"Can I bring anything?" he questioned. "Toys, maybe?
Candy?"

"Oh, no. That's not necessary."

"Are you sure?" he pressed. "I'd be more than glad
to—"

"No. Really, Marty." Donna smiled again. "Your being
there is what's important."

Her last comment triggered something inside Marty. Not
a memory, exactly. More like a tangle of recollected moments and emotions. He stiffened, trying to stave off the
encroachment of the past.

But where is he? a voice inside his head demanded. The
voice belonged to a bewildered little boy. *He said he'd be
here.*

He didn't want to miss your play, a second voice answered. This one belonged to a woman. *But he got sick . . .*

He promised. The first voice. Older. Angrier. *He promised he'd come to the game!*

He wanted to be here. The second voice. Tighter. More
tired. *You know he wanted to be here. But things didn't go
very well at his meeting . . .*

So he didn't show. The first voice again. Almost adult this
time. Almost indifferent. *Big deal. I never expected—*

The sound of his name and the stroke of a hand brought
Marty back to the present. He drew a shuddery breath,
blinking like a man emerging from a nightmare.

"Marty?" Donna repeated softly. She touched his right
forearm for a second time. "Are you all right?"

"Yeah," he said quickly. She'd moved close enough so he
could catch the scent of her perfume. The fragrance was so
fresh. So clean. "Sure. I'm fine. Just a little indigestion
from Rosa's *chilis rellenos.*"

"Oh."

She didn't believe him. He could see it in her steady green
eyes.

"Donna—" he began guiltily.

"I pressed too hard, didn't I?" she asked ruefully. "I'm sorry. Lydia Foster tells me I tend to twist arms when it comes to the Center."

"No," Marty disputed, shaking his head. "It's okay."

"Our kids make some people uncomfortable," she went on determinedly. "They're a reminder of how cruel the world can be. And that's not an easy thing to be reminded of, especially when there seems to be so little we can do about it. So, if that's what's bothering you, and if you want to change your mind about coming on Saturday, I'll understand."

She was offering him an out. Gently. Generously. And without a hint that she was judging him as she did so.

For one galling, gutless instant, Marty considered taking it.

He couldn't.

"I'll be at the Center on Saturday," he said steadily. "I *promise*."

With five years' worth of Celebrity Saturdays under her belt, Donna thought she was prepared for anything. She was wrong. She was in no way prepared for what she felt when she saw Marty making his way across the sun-drenched grounds of the Better Day Center for Children four days later.

Actually, Lydia Foster was the first to spot him. It was shortly before one. The Center was bubbling with activity. She and Donna were sitting behind a balloon-adorned table, greeting guests and handing out name tags the children had made for the visiting celebrities.

"I've only got one question," the psychologist said suddenly.

"What's that?" Donna asked absently, rearranging the remaining name tags. Her fingers lingered briefly on the one she'd lettered herself.

"Exactly what have you been up to that's got Marty Knight looking at you like you're a bowl of cream and he's a hungry tomcat, and why haven't you told me about it?"

Donna's head snapped up. Her heart leapt.

Marty!

It had been four days since she'd seen him. Although they'd talked several times on the phone, it hadn't been the same. She hadn't realized until that instant how much she'd wanted to see him again.

Then again, maybe she *had* realized it—deep down. But she hadn't allowed herself to admit it. Admitting such a thing wasn't in line with the slow-going they'd agreed to.

Marty was dressed very casually—sneakers, a pair of faded jeans that clung to the bottom half of his lean body like plastic wrap, and a torso-hugging white T-shirt. He was moving toward them swiftly, his well-muscled legs eating up the distance in long, lithe strides.

Donna found herself fluffing her breeze-tousled hair. She knew she was blushing, but she didn't care. She got to her feet rather clumsily.

And then Marty was standing on the other side of the table. He was close enough to reach out and touch.

"Hi," he said.

"Hi," she returned throatily. "I'm glad you came."

Marty's features tightened for an instant. Anger flickered through the depths of his dark eyes. "I promised I would, Donna."

She hadn't meant to imply that she'd doubted his word. "No, Marty," she began. "I didn't—I wasn't—"

"Hello," Lydia Foster intervened smoothly, putting out her hand. "I'm Lydia Foster."

Marty's expression cleared. He shifted his attention to Lydia. "The perceptive child psychologist," he identified immediately, taking her hand and shaking it.

Lydia lifted her brows. "I'm flattered, Mr. Knight."

"It's Marty, Dr. Foster. And it wasn't flattery. Donna's told me a lot about you and your work here at the Center."

"It's Lydia, Marty," the other woman returned. Her tone was friendly. "Has Donna told you about me voluntarily? I mean, I've had to pry like crazy to get her to say anything about you."

"Lydia!" Donna gasped, suddenly finding her voice. It was one thing for her friend to hit it off with Marty. It was entirely another to have her entering into an instant alliance with him.

Lydia turned. "Yes, Donna?" she inquired mildly.

"You haven't had to pry like crazy to get me to—" Donna broke off, her cheeks flaming as she realized what kind of inference could be drawn from what she'd just said.

"Then I take it you've been talking about me behind my back?" Marty queried, his voice as bland as butter.

Donna picked up the name tag she'd made for him and extended it. "If you're going to take anything," she said, "take this."

He accepted the name tag and made a show of examining the safety pin taped to the back. "Now why should the phrase 'and stick it' suddenly occur to me?" he wondered wryly.

Lydia started laughing.

After a moment or two, Donna joined in. The tension in the atmosphere dissolved. "Maybe because you're as perceptive as Dr. Foster," she retorted.

Marty grinned and attached the tag to his T-shirt.

"I don't want you to think I thought you weren't going to come today," Donna said seriously a few minutes later. Lydia had waved her and Marty off with smiling assurances that she could handle the task of name-tag distribution without assistance.

Marty took Donna's right hand in his left. A sweet tingle of pleasure ran through her body. Her fingers began to knit with his.

"No problem," he answered. "I'm sorry I was so touchy. Anyway, you had no way of being sure I'd show up."

There it was again. That subtle self-deprecation Donna had noticed several times before. She experienced a flicker of distress, wondering what prompted Marty's apparent impulse to keep putting himself down.

"I don't know about that," she replied. "You gave me your promise."

Marty checked himself in mid-stride. He turned to face her. "And you believed it?"

"I had no reason not to, Marty."

His dark eyes flicked back and forth. "Even though I acted—" he grimaced "—the way I acted when you asked me?"

She nodded.

Marty seemed to weigh her answer carefully. Finally he lifted his free hand and brushed his fingertips against her cheek. "Thank you for believing me."

"You're welcome," she responded, then smiled. "Now, come on. Let me give you the official Celebrity Saturday tour."

The tour didn't last very long. Barely five minutes into it, one of the Center's resident staffers rushed up to inform Donna that the outdoor sound system had broken down.

"Duty calls," Donna said with an apologetic smile.

"I'll see you later," Marty replied with an understanding nod.

The next two hours flew by. There weren't any real emergencies, just an endless series of questions to be answered, decisions to be made, and loose ends to be tied up. The burden of dealing with these problems fell squarely on Donna's shoulders. But she was more than willing to carry the weight, even when it involved trying to coax the Center's newest and least responsive resident into taking part in the day's activities. Coping with young Sam Collins probably required more effort and produced less results than anything else she was called on to do.

It was a few minutes after three-thirty when Donna finally managed to reunite with Marty. She found him sitting at the base of a huge oak tree, surrounded by about a dozen children. He was trading knock-knock jokes with them. Because she'd come up behind him, she couldn't see his expression. But his fluent voice and flexible posture suggested he was a man very much at ease.

There was no doubt that his audience was having a wonderful time.

"Me next! Me next!" the children squealed, waving their hands, vying eagerly for his attention.

"Vell let me zee-ee-ee," Marty said with an exaggerated accent. The youngsters laughed. "Okay, okay." He gestured for order. The children made a show of shushing each other, then quieted down. "Our next knock-knock joke will be told by—"

"Miss Day!" a little girl named Amanda Browne blurted out, pointing a stubby finger at Donna. "Miss Day!"

Donna caught her breath. Amanda Browne was one of the shiest children in residence at the Center. The fact that she was a member of the boisterous group surrounding Marty was remarkable enough. The fact that she'd actually spoken up without prompting was astounding.

The other youngsters took up the cry. "Yeah! Yeah! Miss Day!"

Donna looked at Marty. He'd shifted around and was gazing up at her, his sensually shaped mouth curved into a roguishly expectant smile. The expression in his eyes made her recall Lydia's earlier comment about tomcats and cream.

"I think that's a terrific idea," he declared. He got to his feet in a seamless movement. "Let's have Miss Day tell the next knock-knock joke."

Donna flushed, then slowly moved forward to stand next to Marty. She ran her tongue over her lips, scanning the children's eager, upturned faces.

"You have to say knock-knock, Miss Day," little Amanda piped up.

"Knock, knock," Donna repeated, desperately trying to think of a joke. Lord, she had to know *one!* She was a comedian's daughter!

"Who's there?" the children demanded instantly.

"Uh—uh—"

At that point the Better Day Center for Children's outdoor sound system squealed to life and a voice announced the arrival of the Teenage Mutant Ninja Turtles.

Donna lost her audience—except for Marty—in less than fifteen seconds.

"Lucky break, lady," Marty mocked.

"And what's that supposed to mean?" Donna inquired, tilting her chin.

"It means the Turtles saved your skin. We both know you had no idea where you were going with your knock-knock joke."

"I was improvising."

"Uh-huh. Sure. Pull the other one."

"I suppose you would've let me stand there and bomb."

"Nah. I would've bailed you out." A perfectly calibrated pause, then a wink-punctuated zinger. "Eventually."

"Nasty, Mr. Knight."

"Hey," he shrugged lazily, "I'm a comic, Miss Day."

Donna laughed. "Yes, well, I also think you're a phony."

She'd meant it in jest, of course. But she glimpsed a flash of emotion in Marty's eyes that told her her words had struck home in a very hurtful way.

"Oh?" he asked. In the space of a heartbeat, he'd gone on the defensive. The change was unnerving.

"I was talking about what you said Tuesday night," Donna tried to clarify after an awkward pause. "About not being very good with kids." She ventured a cautious smile. "From where I was standing a few minutes ago, you seemed to be terrific with them."

"Oh." Some of the tension seeped out of his posture. "That."

"Yes, that." She hesitated, then decided to press the issue. "What did you think I was talking about?"

He shrugged again. The movement was as controlled as the previous one had been casual. "I don't know."

"Marty—"

"The kids here aren't what I expected, you know," he interrupted. "Except for the one with the brown eyes and the Marine-style haircut you were talking with about an hour ago. Or maybe talking *at* is a better way to put it. You were putting out, but you didn't seem to be getting much back."

"You mean...Sam Collins?" Donna asked, taken aback. She hadn't forgotten the connection she'd made the first time she'd seen Sam's picture. Indeed, the more she saw of man and boy, the stronger the linkage seemed—whatever the linkage was. That Marty should focus on Sam, out of all the children at the Center...

"Yeah, if Sam Collins is the one with the droopy jeans and the ratty T-shirt," Marty said. "He seems like a tough little—"

He didn't have a chance to finish. The sound system squealed to life once again. This time, it summoned Donna back to work.

"Everything okay?" Lydia Foster asked when Donna came out of the Center's main building a short time later.

"Just fine," Donna answered, glancing around.

The other woman smiled knowingly. "If you're looking for Marty, I saw him just a few—" She broke off, her smile vanishing. Her gaze fixed on something behind Donna.

Alarmed by Lydia's expression, Donna pivoted around.

She turned just in time to see Sam Collins spit in Marty Knight's face.

Six

Sam Collins expected to get hit.

Marty could see the anticipation in the kid's spiky-lashed brown eyes. The message couldn't have been clearer if it had been printed on a billboard.

He'd gotten a grip on the boy's left shoulder a split second after the glob of spittle had hit his cheek. He wasn't gripping hard enough to hurt. He'd cut his hands off before he'd do something like that to a child. But he was holding on firmly enough to make certain the kid got the message that he wasn't going to let go until he was good and ready.

As he'd indicated to Donna, Sam Collins had made quite an impression on him. The boy had stuck out from the Celebrity Saturday crowd like the clichéd sore thumb. If there'd been an organization called Uncuddly Kids Anonymous and it had been looking for a poster child, Sam Collins would have been a prime candidate.

He'd felt vaguely unsettled as he'd watched the skinny, sloppily dressed kid drift around the edges of the Celebrity Saturday activities like a storm cloud. His uneasiness had intensified as he'd seen the boy rebuff at least a half dozen attempts to draw him into the festivities.

Something he'd observed had caught Marty by surprise. Not once had he seen the kid try to ruin anybody's enjoyment of the afternoon. As miserable as he obviously was, the boy didn't seem to begrudge the other children their fun.

And it wasn't a matter of his being indifferent to the fun, either. Marty had the distinct impression that Sam was keenly sensitive to everything going on around him.

Marty also had the definite sense that the boy was very much aware of a certain auburn-haired, green-eyed member of the Center's staff. He'd noticed Sam's brown-eyed gaze darting in Donna Day's direction several times.

His own gaze had traveled toward the same destination on more occasions than he could count.

Marty had deliberately sought Sam out following his aborted conversation with Donna. He wasn't certain why he'd done so. Maybe it had had something to do with the stunned expression he'd seen on Donna's face when he'd mentioned the boy.

In any case, the impulse had grabbed him and he'd gone with it. After a bit of looking, he'd spotted Sam hunkered down on one of the wooden benches scattered around the Center's neatly tended grounds.

He'd approached, seated himself next to the youngster and started talking. He'd anticipated rejection from the start and he'd gotten it . . . right in the face.

You want me to do it, don't you? he thought, meeting the boy's furious stare without wavering. You want me to haul off and whack you because as soon as I do that, we're at the bottom line. And that's what you need, isn't it? You only feel safe when you know exactly how far you can push before it all comes back on you. And when all is said and done, you'd rather get a belt up front than buy into some nice guy bull that turns out to be nothing but crap in the end. Because it hurts the worst when you get slammed after letting your guard down, doesn't it? It hurts the worst because you feel like a chump for having trusted somebody. It hurts the worst because it feels like it's all your fault.

At that point Donna and Lydia Foster rushed up.

"Marty—"

"Sam—"

Marty held his left hand up like a traffic cop. He knew how Sam would interpret the gesture. The kid's flinch sliced into him like a knife.

I won't hit you, Sam, he thought. No matter what you do, I won't hit you.

Marty didn't bother offering the assurance aloud. He realized that the person it was meant for would never believe it.

"Everything's cool, ladies," he said calmly. He wiped the saliva off his cheek with a quick pass of his fingers, then brought his left hand back down to his side. "Sam was just giving me his opinion on my personal hygiene."

The boy's brown eyes flicked back and forth. It was obvious he didn't understand the last word Marty had used. It was equally obvious he didn't know what to make of Marty's apparently laid-back attitude.

Pale, pinched features contorted without warning. "You stink!" Sam hissed. "You stink like sh—." He used a four-letter word.

"Like sh—?" Marty lobbed the word right back. He had a fleeting memory of having had his mouth washed out with soap for having spoken the same expletive more than two decades before. "That bad?"

"Worse!"

"Really? Geez. I took a shower before I came. I used underarm deodorant, too. Maybe it's my hair. I started using this new shampoo not too long ago, so it could be that. Or maybe it's my breath. What do you think? Hair? Breath? General B.O.?"

"Leave me alone!" The boy tried to jerk away.

Out of the corner of his eye, Marty saw Donna start to take a step forward. He also saw Lydia catch her by the arm. The woman shook her head in a barely perceptible movement. Donna went very still.

"Come on," he urged, maintaining his grip on the boy. "You've got to help me out here. I've been going around this place for the last three hours or so stinking like—" he used the word again "—and nobody's said a word. Then I happen to sit down next to the one person who's got the guts to tell me the truth. Do you know how embarrassed I feel? I mean, I strolled right up to—'' he named the macho star of a successful TV action series ''—earlier and introduced myself. He gave me this dirty look and walked away. I figured he was just being stuck up, you know? But now I realize I must have offended him. There's no telling how many people I've offended today.''

Sam dipped his fair-haired head, burrowing his chin into his narrow chest. ''He's not such a big deal,'' he muttered after nearly ten seconds.

''Who?'' Marty asked.

The boy looked up, his chin jutting. ''That guy you just said.'' He repeated the name disdainfully. ''He's not such a big deal.''

''He's on TV.''

The boy snorted derisively. ''His show's a total gyp and he's a big phony. He doesn't do any of that stuff, you know. Like crashing up cars and jumping out of airplanes. No way he does any of that! And anyway. Why should you care if he's on TV? You're on TV, too. You're that weird guy, John Doe. You're on *Murphy's Law.*''

''You've seen *Murphy's Law?*'' Marty had suspected Sam had recognized him when he'd sat down, but he hadn't pressed the issue. He'd learned that having a famous face could be a two-edged sword.

The boy's expression turned wary, as if he'd just realized he'd been maneuvered into talking when he hadn't intended to. He waited a few moments, then shrugged indifferently. ''Yeah.''

Marty lifted his hand from Sam's shoulder. ''What do you think?''

Another shrug. ''It's okay, I guess.'' A scowl. ''That lawyer—the one who gives you the jobs delivering those papers . . . he's stupid.''

''You mean Francis Murphy?''

''Yeah. Him. Murphy.''

''He's the star.''

''No, sir.''

''Yes, sir.''

"No way!"

"Hey, kid, the show's called *Murphy's Law*. The actor who plays Murphy has to be the star."

"But nobody watches because of him!" Sam insisted fiercely. "They watch because of you! You always get the most claps when you come on. Like that time, a couple of weeks ago, when you went into the courtroom wearing that gorilla suit. Boy, the audience really—"

"You want to talk about stinking?" Marty interpolated. "I think there must've been a family of *skunks* living in that suit before I put it on. Let me tell you, it was P.U. City."

There was a pause.

Sam squirmed for a second or two, then scratched the tip of his nose. Marty saw his brown eyes dart toward Donna and Lydia.

"'Magine—" the boy's throat worked several times "—'magine if they were still in there."

It was a joke. It was a small one, offered very hesitantly, but it was a joke nonetheless.

Marty chuckled. Not a lot. He knew Sam wouldn't buy a big belly laugh and he had no intention of insulting the kid by forcing one. He chuckled just enough to make it clear he appreciated the humor in the remark.

And then he realized that Donna was laughing, too. The sound of her laughter was soft and rippling. It twisted around his nervous system like a satin ribbon. Teasing him. Tantalizing him. Tying him into knots.

His reaction was so strong he was afraid she was overdoing it. Then he understood that such a thing was impossible. Donna didn't fake her laughter. It either came from her heart or it didn't come at all.

Marty saw a series of emotions sleet through the depths of Sam's eyes. It was spooky to watch them. They were going by too quickly to count or categorize, yet he knew them as though they were his own.

The left corner of Sam's mouth quirked, just for an instant.

Marty cleared his throat. "Skunks still in the gorilla suit, huh?" he echoed. "That's really a disgusting thought,

Sam." He pumped his voice full of guy-to-guy admiration, the kind no girl could every truly understand.

The left corner of Sam's mouth quirked again. "Yeah," he admitted with a hint of pride. "Pretty gross."

There was another pause.

"You hungry?" Marty asked eventually. He kept his tone casual.

Sam shrugged, reverting to indifference. "You?"

"Kind of."

"They were cookin' burgers before."

"Feel like getting one?"

"With you?"

This time, Marty shrugged.

Sam considered the offer. Finally he nodded. "Okay."

Marty stood up. He glanced at Donna and Lydia. Donna was staring at him, eyes wide, lips slightly parted. She was looking at him as if she'd never seen him before. Lydia was staring at him, too. She was smiling.

"Excuse us, ladies," he requested.

"Yeah," Sam said in an identical manner. He got up from the bench, too. "'Scuze us, ladies."

The finish of a Celebrity Saturday usually found Donna teetering between exhilaration and exhaustion. This Celebrity Saturday was no exception. But added to the volatile mix was a sense of wonderment.

She'd been telling the truth earlier in the week when she'd said she thought Marty was underestimating himself with his assertion that he wasn't very good with kids. Even so, she'd never expected he'd be able to...

She glanced at the man moving so easily beside her. They were walking toward the Center's parking lot. Marty had a one-night stand at The Funny Farm ahead of him. A warm-up, he'd explained, for the Las Vegas gig he had scheduled for June. She, on the other hand, faced a staff review of the day's events. That had been the reason she'd turned down his suggestion that she come to see him perform.

Or, at least, that's the reason she'd given him. The truth was, she needed to be by herself. She needed time to sort through the discoveries she'd made during the past few hours.

She couldn't stop thinking about the way Marty had handled Sam Collins. No. Not *handled* him. The idea of handling implied manipulation. Marty's dealings with Sam Collins had been anything but manipulative. They'd appeared to have been utterly instinctive. He'd seemed to know—at some profound, unspoken level—exactly what to do and how to do it. And Sam had responded to him. Lord! How he had responded.

Marty exhaled on a long, sighing breath.

"Tired?" Donna asked softly.

He looked at her. She had the feeling he'd been a million miles away. "Why do you ask?"

"The kids can take a lot out of you if you're not used to them."

He ran a hand through his hair. "I'd imagine they can do that even if you are."

"True," she conceded.

They walked a bit more.

Then—

"His old man whacks him around, doesn't he." It wasn't a question. And there was no need for Marty to identify the "him."

Donna stopped. Marty did the same. "Sam told you that?" she asked urgently, staring up into his face.

He shook his head as though trying to clear it. "You don't tell things like that," he responded in an odd tone.

The sentence sounded like a non sequitur, but Donna's instincts told her it wasn't. A chill shivered down her spine. "Marty—" she began.

"He does, doesn't he?"

There was a seal of confidentiality Donna couldn't breach. "Sam's never admitted his father's abused him," she replied carefully.

Marty didn't push her on the matter. "The guy's in jail, right?"

That, at least, was a matter of public record. "Yes. For drunken driving."

Marty's mouth twisted. "Now why doesn't that surprise me?"

After a moment he resumed walking. Donna followed him. There was silence between them until they reached his car.

"Look," Marty turned to face her once again. "I had a chance to talk with some of the people who were here today." He paused.

"And?" Donna prompted after a few seconds.

"And...I understand you've got volunteers who come to see the kids even when it isn't Celebrity Saturday."

She realized what was coming. "That's right," she affirmed slowly.

"How, uh—" he gestured "—how would you feel about my dropping by?"

Donna averted her face slightly, searching for a way to phrase the things she knew she had to say. She could feel the weight of Marty's scrutiny. God! Four days earlier, he'd resisted the notion of visiting the Center for a single afternoon. Now he was offering to "drop by"...on a regular basis! If Sam Collins was the reason for his change of—

"Donna." Marty captured her chin between thumb and forefinger. With gentle but inexorable pressure, he turned her face toward his. "It's not just Sam. I don't have some sick idea of showing up and playing substitute daddy for him. I want to come for *all* the kids I saw today. I know singling one of them out would end up hurting more than helping. And I wouldn't do that. Please. Believe me. I wouldn't do that."

She believed him. From the very bottom of her heart, she believed him. But she also knew this belief was far from objective. She was deeply attracted to Marty Knight. And the attraction seemed to be growing, exponentially, with each passing moment.

The possibility that this attraction might be clouding her judgment was dangerously real. The danger to herself was one thing. She was an adult. She took responsibility for her actions. But the danger to the children at the Center...

"Are you sure you want to commit the time?" she finally asked.

Marty stroked a knuckle down her throat, then withdrew his hand. "You mean, can you trust me to be here when I say I'll be here?"

She winced inwardly at the bluntness of his question. "Our kids need certainty in their lives, Marty."

"Everybody needs certainty." He let a few seconds tick by. Donna could sense his body tensing, his brain focusing. Finally he continued speaking. His voice was tightly controlled. "It's not easy to keep promises, Donna. That's why I don't make very many of them. But when I do make one, I keep it. And if you and Lydia and whoever else has a say in the matter decide it's all right for me to come to the Center, I promise I won't give you any cause to regret it. I *promise.*"

"In that case," Donna replied after a moment, "I'd be very happy if you'd like to drop by again."

Then, surrendering to impulse, she went up on tiptoe and brushed her lips against his. At the same time she lifted a hand to cup the side of his face. She stroked him gently, the faint stubble of beard growth tickling her skin. She felt the sudden clench of his jaw muscles in response to her touch.

For a moment, maybe two, Marty remained unyielding. But when the change came, it was so complete it stole her breath away.

His mouth opened, then coaxed hers to do the same. His tongue glided over her lips in a suggestive movement. Sampling. Savoring. His arms came around her, drawing her close, holding her tight.

The kiss was slower and sweeter than the one they'd shared eight days before. The heat was there, but it was banked ... at least temporarily. The wildfire eroticism that had ignited so unexpectedly at her front door deferred to the tenderest kind of intimacy.

She murmured his name. Her fingers slid backward from his jaw, winnowing sensuously through his hair. She drank in the sound of her own name being evoked on a husky male whisper. She reveled in the caressing movements of strong, sure hands over her body.

Finally they eased apart. Pulses thrumming. Senses hazed. There was another kiss. Quick, yet clinging. Hot and heady with honeyed implications of pleasures to come.

They separated.

Marty eyed Donna for several seconds. His breathing was uneven when he spoke. "About a week ago...you said you might like to lounge around my house at the beach...with me. Would you still like to?"

Donna nodded.

"How does tomorrow sound?"

It sounded terrific and she told him so.

A languid sigh. "I was wrong."

A leisurely chuckle. "You? Never."

"No, really, Marty." Donna took a sip from the glass of mineral water she was holding. "I told you you should move back from the beach so you could eat at Rosa's more often. Remember?"

"Uh-huh." Marty drank from his own glass of mineral water. "And that was wrong?"

"Mmm." Donna nodded. She set her glass down on the arm of the chaise longue in which she was sitting.

"How so?"

"Well, Rosa's is great. But *this*—" she gestured with a graceful sweep of one arm "—this is heaven."

Marty was deeply pleased by her response, but he feigned nonchalance. "It's okay, I guess."

Donna removed the sunglasses she was wearing. She examined him as if he'd sprouted a second head. "Okay?" she repeated with delicate sarcasm. "You guess?"

"Well..." He let his gaze roam for a few moments, then returned it to the woman sitting barely two yards away from him. He proceeded to conduct a very thorough visual inventory of her.

Shell-pink toenails. Narrow, elegantly arched feet. Slender ankles.

A long, sleek expanse of legs that looked as though they'd been sculpted to wear sheer silk stockings with seams.

The long-sleeved, terry-cloth robe that covered Donna from the smooth start of her upper thighs to the base of her slender throat might have deterred another man. But Marty was more than capable of visualizing what the bulky garment hid. He'd gotten quite an eyeful earlier when he and Donna had frolicked in the surf like a couple of children.

By a lot of standards—especially the three-postage-stamps-tied-together-with-string standard attire that seemed to apply on most California beaches—the one-piece black maillot Donna was wearing beneath her robe was modest to the point of being prudish. But when he thought about the way that modest suit clung once it had gotten wet...

Marty took another drink. A piece of ice bumped against his front teeth. He fleetingly considered fishing it out and applying it to the hotly insistent throb between his thighs.

Donna's gently curving hips. Sweetly rounded bottom...slim waist.

Her small but beautifully formed breasts. Breasts he knew, without ever having caressed them, would fit perfectly in the palms of his hands.

Another drink of mineral water.

Well, no. Not a drink. A gulp.

Onward and upward...so to speak.

Graceful neck. Piquantly sharp chin.

Ripe, rosy lips—parted slightly to reveal a hint of even white teeth.

The nose, endearingly smeared with zinc oxide ointment and flanked by blush-stained cheeks.

The gold-flecked green eyes...

"Well...what?" Donna demanded in a voice that was about an octave higher than normal. She was amazed she could say anything at all. How in the name of heaven had Marty done it? she wondered. How, simply by looking at her, had he brought her to quivering awareness of every inch of her body?

"What?" he repeated blankly. Then, abruptly, he realized what she was talking about. "Oh. I was just going to say that I *have* noticed an improvement in the scenery around here. A very...recent...improvement."

Donna picked up her glass from the arm of the chaise and took a deep drink. "I see."

She saw even more a moment later when Marty got up from his lounge chair and stretched.

It wasn't that the swimsuit he was wearing was skimpy. In point of fact, the low-riding garment was fashioned in the baggy style affected by many surfers. But even so...

His legs were long and lean, toned for endurance. There was athletic power there, but without bulk or bulges.

It didn't matter that the generous cut of his swimsuit obscured the taut swell of his buttocks. Donna had a vivid comprehension of what the garishly colored fabric hid. After all, she'd seen Marty in a pair of jeans.

His belly was washboard flat, punctuated by the shallow indentation of his navel and bisected by a fine line of dark down. His smoothly muscled chest was whorled with more dark hair. The medal Sister Mary Pauline had given him shone in the late afternoon sun every time he inhaled.

Strong, squared shoulders. Proudly set neck and head.

Mobile mouth—curling provocatively at the corners.

Tough-looking nose not quite on plumb.

Bold brown eyes—

"Yes?" Marty queried carefully, meeting Donna's gaze.

He wouldn't have thought it possible for her to flush any more deeply than she already had, but she did. He heard her draw a shuddery little breath, saw her drain off the ounce or so of liquid remaining in her glass.

"I don't know what the scenery around here was like before," she said throatily. "But it seems very...impressive...today."

Marty's blood was simmering. A few more minutes of this and it would be on full rolling boil.

That sounded good to him.

Or...did it?

Too soon? Marty asked himself suddenly, his eyes slewing toward the sliding doors that connected the deck and the house. He knew where they were heading. He knew Donna did, too. There was no question that the speed limit they'd set on their relationship had been raised, if not removed altogether, when she'd accepted his invitation to spend the day at the beach. Nonetheless ...

He'd spoken the truth when he'd told Donna that he'd gone the hit-and-run route with sex in the past. He'd never had any problems handling what he sometimes thought of as the "during" part of male-female relationships. Physical intimacy was fine. It was the "before" and "after" parts—*especially* the "after" part!—he'd always had trouble dealing with.

Marty realized he'd have to deal with the before and after if he and Donna became lovers. More than that, he realized he truly *wanted* to deal with them. But could he? Was he capable of it? What if he tried and discovered he—

"Marty?"

Marty returned to reality with a jolt. He had no idea how long he'd been standing there, lost in a labyrinth of thought. Nor did he have the foggiest notion whether any of what had been going through his head had shown on his face.

He rubbed his chest with the flat of one hand, his fingers tangling briefly in the chain he'd worn around his neck for nineteen years. Too soon, he decided abruptly. Too soon and too fast.

He focused on the glass Donna was still holding. "Uh, yeah," he said, summoning up a smile he hoped didn't look as artificial as it felt. "I thought I'd go in and get us some refills."

"R-refills?" she repeated blankly.

He nodded. "Your glass looks pretty empty to me."

Donna glanced down, vaguely registering that the object in her hand was, indeed, virtually empty.

"Well, uh, yes," she agreed disjointedly. Her thoughts seemed to be flapping around inside her brain like frightened starlings.

"I can offer you something stronger than mineral water."

"Stronger?"

"Yeah. I think I've got some beer stashed away someplace—"

She stiffened. "No."

"I could always pop the cork on the champagne Barry Cooperman—"

"*No.*"

There was a jagged pause.

Marty suddenly recalled what the waiter at The Funny Farm had said about Donna's order. He also recalled her smiling refusal of Emilio's suggestion of a margarita at La Cocina de Rosa. "You don't drink, either?"

Donna asked herself later if she would have picked up on that "either" if she hadn't been so off-balance. She also asked herself if she would have said what she said next if she had.

She never formulated a conclusive response to either question.

"Not anymore," she replied.

Marty's eyes narrowed at her tone. "But you used to?"

"Yes. I used to drink, but not anymore."

He took two steps toward the chaise where she was sitting. "You . . . had a problem?"

Donna set her glass down on the arm of the deck chair. The rattle of the half-melted ice cubes it contained seemed very loud to her.

"I *have* a problem," she corrected, meeting Marty's gaze evenly. "I'm an . . . alcoholic."

Marty realized he'd been holding his breath. He released it in a rushing hiss. He sank down on the end of Donna's chaise. "You?"

She nodded.

He shook his head, denying the possibility. "No." He shook his head again. "No, Donna. You're not the type."

You're not the type.

The words seemed to reverberate in Donna's brain. How many variations on that theme had she heard? she wondered. How many variations had she, herself, used during the years she'd spent lying about her addiction?

"Alcoholics come in every possible size, shape and sex, Marty."

He shook his head a third time. His body was rigid, as if braced for a blow.

"It's true," she insisted.

Anger—as intense as it was unwanted—welled up inside Marty. It chewed at him like a rabid animal. Dangerous.

Destructive. He clenched his hands, trying to fight it down, trying to fight it off.

The anger won.

"Dammit, Donna, *drunks* don't laugh the way you do!"

Donna flinched at his tone, not his words. Lord knew, she'd branded herself far worse than *drunk* in the past.

Marty saw her pained expression. His anger died as swiftly as it had flared, leaving him feeling slightly sick. Remorse and shame surged up to replace the rage.

Suddenly he was a child again. He was small and he was scared. He would have traded his soul to be big and brave... and anywhere but where he was.

What did you call me? a voice inside Marty's skull demanded.

He didn't mean it, another voice said placatingly. *Honey, please. Don't be mad. He didn't mean it. He's just a little upset because you promised—*

Oh, so he's upset, izzy? the first voice slurred. *Well, whudabou' me, huh? I work like a slave for this family and I'm supposed to take this kind of talk? Call me a drunk, will you? C'mere, you lil—*

He didn't mean it! The placating voice turned panicky. *Please, don't—Marty! Marty, you bad boy. See what you've done? Say you're sorry to your father. Say you're sorry, right—*

"I'm sorry," Marty said, stricken. "Donna, I'm so sorry. I didn't mean—God. I'm sorry."

There was a long, long pause.

"No," Donna said finally. She wanted to lean forward and touch Marty, but something in his terribly conflicted expression warned her off. "I'm the one who's sorry. I've obviously made you uncomfortable, Marty. I never intended—"

"No. Don't," Marty interrupted sharply. He started to reach for her but aborted the gesture. His hands were trembling. He stilled them by sheer force of will. "Please. Don't apologize to me, Donna. I was way out of line a minute ago. It's just that what you said..."

He stopped, desperately searching for an acceptable way to explain his reaction. His normal facility for language seemed to have deserted him. He also knew this was not the kind of situation he could salvage with a joke...even if he could come up with one.

"It's just that what I said shocked you."

Marty matched her words against the emotions churning within him. I don't need this, he thought. I don't need this one bit!

Yet he knew he couldn't turn his back and walk away from it. He knew he couldn't turn his back and walk away from Donna.

"Yeah," he admitted. "I mean, I never would have figured you for a—" He gestured, then fell back on the only words that seemed safe to say. "I'm sorry."

There was another pause. Donna was greatly tempted to let the matter drop, to try to recapture the teasing, tantalizing harmony they'd enjoyed for so much of this day. She knew Marty would be willing to follow her lead if that's the path she chose. It would be such an easy way out...

But she wouldn't—she *couldn't*—do it. Donna Elizabeth Day had stopped taking the easy way out nearly twelve years ago. Taking the easy way out meant evading the truth. Taking the easy way out meant avoiding—or trying to alter—reality. In the long run, taking the easy way out exacted an infinitely heavier toll than hanging tough.

"Was it what I said that shocked you?" she questioned. "Or the fact that I said it?"

Marty didn't respond right away. He didn't want to respond, period. But he understood that he had to.

"Both," he answered, forcing himself to look directly into Donna's eyes. He cleared his throat. "How can you say you *have* a problem if you don't drink?"

"I don't drink *anymore,*" she emphasized. "I'm a recovering alcoholic, Marty. Even though I've been sober for nearly twelve years—"

"Twelve years?" That couldn't be right!

"Well, actually, it's eleven years, eleven months, two weeks and three days," Donna conceded with a crooked smile. "But who's counting?"

"Twelve years?" Marty repeated. He remembered Zeke Peters mentioning something about Donna having had a

rocky time during her teens. Marty had figured that he'd meant a few episodes of adolescent rebellion. But *alcoholism?*

"I took my first drink of hard liquor when I was thirteen. I didn't like the taste, but I loved the buzz. And I went on loving it. The problem was, I had to keep increasing my intake to get the same buzz. I cracked up the brand new convertible I got for my Sweet Sixteen because I was driving drunk. And I—I had my first blackout about a year after that."

"Didn't anyone notice? Didn't anyone do anything to help you?"

"I didn't want help. I didn't think I needed it. At least, not then. As for people noticing ... well, they didn't think I was *the type,* either. And I was very careful. Very clever. Except for the time with the car. That was criminally stupid. But I lied through my teeth and ended up getting away with it."

"What about your parents?" he demanded. "Where were they?"

"My mother died when I was nine. And Donnie was wrapped up in his career. He was on the road a lot. I was away at boarding school. I made it a point to get good grades. I usually made it a point to drink alone too. Except for the last few months, I didn't party with other people very much."

"The last few months?"

Donna hesitated for a moment. Memories assailed her. She didn't try to turn away from them. Denial didn't do any good. The past, ignored, tended to fester in the ugliest possible way. The past, admitted and understood, could set a person free.

"The last few months before I finally hit bottom," she clarified quietly.

Before I finally hit bottom.

Marty didn't know how to interpret the way Donna said these last five words. Certainly the image they evoked was a terrible one. Yet her voice and expression were serene with acceptance when she spoke them.

"What happened?" He had to ask. He had to know.

For the first time since she'd initiated this exchange, Donna lowered her gaze. She fingered the left cuff of her robe, acutely conscious of the thudding rhythm of her heartbeat and the in-out pattern of her breathing. There'd been a time when she'd believed she wanted no more of either. She still bore the scars of that time ... of that desperately misguided belief.

Donna lifted her eyes to meet Marty's once again.

"What happened was, I realized I wanted to live," she said simply. "And I found a way to do it, one day at a time."

Marty shifted. He forked a hand back through his hair. He shifted again. He felt—what? he asked himself. Exactly what was it he was feeling at this moment? He sure as hell was feeling something!

He had no doubt there was a phrase—some succinctly specific combination of words—to sum up what was going on inside him. Unfortunately, he had no idea what it was.

Then again ... maybe he did, but he wasn't ready to face it.

Donna, on the other hand, seemed to him to be ready to face just about anything. Maybe that's why she could laugh the way she did. She hadn't been born with that healthy, heartfelt laugh, he decided. She'd earned it.

"Are you always so up-front about this?" he eventually inquired. In the course of the shifting he'd done, he'd closed much of the distance between them.

Donna flushed a little. "No," she confessed. "Not always. Not even usually."

He ran his tongue over his lips. "Why did you tell me?"

Donna felt the heat in her cheeks increase by several degrees. "I wanted you to know. I—it seemed right for me to tell you."

"And now that you have?"

Donna glanced away for a moment, then looked back. "It's up to you, Marty."

Marty reached forward. He took her right hand and lifted it to his lips. He brushed his mouth against her knuckles.

"No, Donna," he said with quiet conviction. "It's up to us."

It's up to us.

Four simple words, yet they possessed the power to move Donna Day to the very marrow of her bones.

It's up to us.

To us.

To him and her.

To the two of them . . . together.

It's up to us.

It was nearly two weeks before Donna understood how hard it must have been for Marty to hear her admission of alcoholism, then offer her the emotional assurance of those four simple words.

Seven

———

Sam Collins squirmed.

Sam Collins scowled.

Sam Collins folded his skinny arms across his skinny, T-shirted chest, putting up a barrier against the world in general and the woman sitting opposite him in particular. Even his fair, short hair seemed to bristle with resistance.

"Can I go now, Miss Day?" he demanded, repeating the question he'd asked at least six times already.

Donna stole a surreptitious glance at the brightly banded watch that encircled her left wrist. The time blocked out for this counseling session was almost up. She felt the encounter had been productive. If nothing else, Sam had stayed put for almost the full sixty minutes.

"What are you going to do if I say yes, Sam?" she inquired.

The boy's brown eyes narrowed. "What do you care?"

Donna didn't allow herself to be baited into telling her prickly young counselee the truth, which was that she cared a great deal. Like most of the children at the Center, Sam Collins suffered from a desperate lack of self-esteem. Because of this, his first instinct was to mistrust people who asserted that what he felt or said or did mattered to them. Because he put such little value on himself, he found it virtually impossible to believe that anyone else would classify him as worthy of time or attention. Words would not change his mind. Only actions could accomplish that.

"I'm just curious," she answered evenly. "You've been trying to get out of here ever since you walked in. I figure you must have something interesting on your schedule."

Sam snorted. "Oh, yeah. Right. Like there's so much interesting stuff to do around this place." He glared at Donna, challenging her to dispute this sarcastic assessment.

"If you say so," she returned, matching his belligerent gaze with a calm one.

"Well, I do!"

"That's fine, Sam. You're entitled to your opinion."

"Yeah, but you think my 'pinion's stupid!"

"No, I don't. I may not agree with your opinion, but I certainly don't think it's stupid." Donna paused for a moment, then asked, "Would it bother you if I thought your opinion was stupid?"

Two weeks before, Sam's response to a similar question had been fast and furious. He'd made it clear to Donna that he couldn't care less what she thought about anything. But now...

The youngster shrugged.

"Would it make you feel sad?"

A second shrug, accompanied by a grimace of disdain.

"How about mad? Do you think it would make you feel mad?"

Sam stiffened. "I'm not stupid!"

"I know that," Donna emphasized swiftly, not missing the youngster's refusal to admit to his capacity for experiencing anger. For all his aggressive behavior, Sam Collins was frightened of the fury he had burning inside him. Donna understood that he was frightened of it because he couldn't allow himself to direct it at the one person who truly deserved it—his father. "Believe me, Sam. I know you're not stupid. As a matter of fact, I think you're very smart."

There was a short, sharp silence, punctuated by the sound of Sam drawing a shuddery breath. "I don't want to talk to you anymore today," he announced abruptly.

Donna weighed her options. Sam's use of the word *today* struck her as a positive sign. The youngster had begun their first counseling session with the declaration that he didn't want to talk to her about anything *ever*.

"All right," she agreed.

Sam responded as though she'd done just the opposite. "You said I could stop when I wanted to," he insisted, arguing a point she'd already conceded.

"That's right, I did," Donna affirmed patiently. "And I meant it. If you don't feel like talking anymore today, we'll stop. We can talk again on Monday."

Sam studied Donna silently for several seconds, plainly wondering whether her acquiescence to his wishes was some kind of trick. She clamped down on a sudden rush of anger at the circumstances that had deprived a ten-year-old boy of the ability to trust another human being.

"Is that okay with you, Sam?" she asked. One of the things Donna tried to do for the children she dealt with was offer them a sense that they had some say in their lives. She wanted them to learn to think of themselves as people with rights and responsibilities, not as pawns or victims. "Is it okay if we talk again on Monday?"

A few more seconds ticked by. Finally, Sam unfolded his arms. He shifted around in his seat. "Yeah," he muttered unenthusiastically, plucking at the front of his T-shirt. "I guess."

"Good."

"So, can I go?" He wiped his nose with the back of his hand.

"Uh-huh."

Sam got up and headed for the door. A step before reaching it, he pivoted back to face Donna. Something about his expression made her brace herself.

"Do you know Marty Knight really good?" he blurted out.

Somehow, Donna managed not to blush. Sam's blunt inquiry had an unnervingly familiar ring to it. She'd been asking herself a similar—if more grammatically correct—question at increasingly frequent intervals during the past fourteen days and nights.

Did she *really* know Marty Knight?

There were moments when Donna would have answered yes. Yes, absolutely. How could she not "really know" a man who made her feel the way Marty Knight did?

And yet . . .

And yet, for every moment when she would have answered yes, she really knew Marty Knight, Donna recognized that there was at least one other when she would have been forced to say no, she didn't know him at all. The man who could stir her so intimately was capable of turning into a stranger in the space of a single heartbeat.

The flexible grace of his body would stiffen into a posture that was both defiant and defensive.

Wariness would extinguish the expressive brilliance of his brown eyes.

His resonant voice would flatten. His usually unfettered flow of words would become a sharply controlled trickle.

Donna could make some educated guesses about the root causes of these sudden shifts in Marty's manner, of course. She was, after all, a trained observer of human behavior. But guessing wasn't knowing and knowing wasn't something she could accomplish all by herself. The only way she could—

"Do you, Miss Day?" Sam repeated.

Donna blinked. "Marty and I are friends, Sam," she replied after a second or two.

"Is that how come he comes here?"

"You mean, is he doing me a favor?"

"Yeah. Or like, is he tryin' to impress you?"

Donna recognized the insecurity that had prompted Sam to broach this issue. She also recognized how careful she had to be in offering him the reassurance he was seeking.

"Marty decided to come back to the Center after he visited here on Celebrity Saturday," she said. "It was his idea. He's not doing it as a favor to me. He's doing it because he wants to. As for trying to impress me—he was here Sunday afternoon, wasn't he?"

Sam nodded emphatically.

"But I wasn't, was I?" She'd wanted to be, but she'd had a long-standing commitment to attend a party honoring one of the Center's most generous patrons.

Sam hesitated for an instant, then shook his head.

"Well, if Marty Knight was trying to impress me, it'd be pretty dumb of him to show up when I wasn't here, don't you think?"

Sam furrowed his forehead, mulling this over. "Yeah," he finally concurred, his expression easing a bit. "Pretty dumb."

"So—"

"He's not comin' here 'cause of pu'licity, either, you know," Sam volunteered.

Donna frowned. "What do you mean?"

"Well, *some* of the bigshots who show up at C'lebrity Saturday only care about posin' for pictures and talkin' to the reporters. I guess they want to make people think they're saints or something. But you can tell they're big fakers. Like, they don't really mean that goofy stuff they say. And they only smile with their teeth, not with their eyes. Anyways, when me and Marty went to get a burger—'member?—this camera guy came up to us. And he was about to start clickin' away when Marty gave him this really wicked look. So the camera guy says, 'What's the problem?' And Marty says, 'No pictures without permission.' So the camera guy kind of whines and says, 'Can I take a picture, Marty?' And Marty says, 'Don't ask me, ask him.'" Sam drew himself up, puffed his chest out and cocked his chin. "And he meant me, Miss Day! Marty meant the camera guy had to ask *me* for permission."

"Which was exactly right, considering you were going to be in the picture," Donna assured him. "What happened then?"

Sam's momentary flash of exuberance fizzled. His chin dropped. He seemed to shrink into himself. "I told him he couldn't take any pictures of me and Marty," he concluded tightly. "I told him—I told him my dad wouldn't like it."

Donna fought to keep her expression neutral. "I see."

"Havin' a picture of me and Marty would've been okay," the boy admitted after a few seconds. "But if it got in a newspaper or somethin'..." He gestured awkwardly, his voice trailing off into unhappy silence.

"I understand, Sam."

Sam gave her an anxious look. "Marty didn't mind that I told the camera guy to go away."

"I'm sure he didn't."

"Like I said, he wasn't out for pu'licity, you know? 'Course he gets lots. Just a couple of days ago, I saw this magazine that had a story about him. It had a big picture of his house at the beach. Have you gone there?"

Donna hesitated. "Ah, yes," she answered cautiously. "Once."

"Is it nice?"

"Very."

"Yeah." Sam nodded solemnly. "I figured."

There was a short pause.

"Sam—"

"I'm gonna go now," the youngster cut her off. "You said I could."

Donna suppressed a sigh. She could tell by Sam's expression that he was determined to leave. "All right. I'll see you on Monday."

"'Bye."

"'Bye."

For once, Sam didn't slam the door on his way out.

Lydia Foster dropped by a few minutes later.

"I just saw Sam Collins," she announced as she walked into Donna's office.

Donna looked up from one of the seemingly endless series of state-mandated forms she had to keep current. The staff at the Center theorized that these forms were endowed with supernatural powers of reproduction. Leave two documents from the child welfare bureaucracy in an In basket overnight, the black-humored claim went, and there would be four documents the next morning.

"Oh?" Donna asked with a tinge of anxiety.

"He told me a riddle," Lydia said.

"Really?"

"Uh-huh. How can you tell a happy motorcycle rider?"

"I have no idea."

"Neither did I. But according to Sam, you can tell by the squished bugs on his teeth."

Donna smiled. "Gross."

"I said the same thing, which seemed to please him to no end." Lydia paused, her expression turning thoughtful. "I think Sam's making progress."

"He's beginning to open up a little," Donna agreed. "But it's definitely two steps forward and one step back with him."

"I know how that is," Lydia declared feelingly. "Look, I can see you're up to your elbows in paperwork. I just stopped by to ask if you could float me a small loan. The damned automated teller machine ate my bank card this morning and I'm temporarily tapped out."

"Oh, sure. My wallet's somewhere in my shoulder bag." Donna gestured. "It's there. Hanging on the back of the door. You'll have to root around a little. You know how much stuff I carry around. Take whatever you need."

"Thanks."

"No problem." Donna went back to filling out forms.

A few moments went by.

"Well, well, well," Lydia said suddenly. "I guess this answers one of the questions I've been biting my tongue to keep from asking you."

Donna glanced up. "What—?" she began, then broke off abruptly as she realized what the "this" her friend had referred to was.

"I'm relieved to know you and Marty are practicing safe sex," Lydia went on, flourishing a small, foil-wrapped packet.

Donna flushed. She'd put that packet—and several others like it—in her carryall shortly before she'd driven off to spend the day "lounging around" at the beach with Marty. She'd understood there was every possibility that the lounging around would blossom into lovemaking, and she'd wanted to be prepared. She hadn't allowed herself to be coy or casual about it. She was, after all, an adult woman, not an innocent or ignorant girl.

Even so...

"Donna?"

Donna forced herself to meet her friend's disconcertingly direct gaze. Her cheeks felt hot enough to fry eggs on. "No," she managed to say. "I, we, uh, we're not."

Lydia looked genuinely shocked. She crossed to Donna's desk, still holding the condom packet. "Don't tell me," she said, placing the prophylactic on the edge of the desk in a very deliberate manner, "you're not practicing because you've got it perfect, right?"

Donna hesitated for a moment, then shook her head. "We're not practicing, period."

There was a long pause.

Finally, Lydia sank into the chair Sam Collins had vacated a short time before. "Boy, is my face red," she said.

Donna smiled crookedly. "Not as red as mine."

"Donna, I'm sorry. I never meant—"

"It's all right."

"It's just that after I saw the sparks the two of you were producing at Celebrity Saturday, I naturally assumed—"

"It's all right, Lydia."

The other woman frowned, obviously trying to formulate some new assumptions. "You've been out with Marty—what?—seven or eight times?"

Donna veiled her eyes with her lashes and twiddled a lock of hair. Her heart was thudding like a drum. The color in her cheeks was still very high.

To talk, or not to talk...

It wasn't even a question. She needed someone to confide in, to counsel with. She'd needed someone for days. And she knew Lydia Foster, Ph.D., was the best someone she could find.

"Nine," she admitted without elaboration. It would be ten times tomorrow evening when Marty escorted her to an end-of-the-season party being hosted by Arnold Golding.

"Nine?" Under different circumstances, Lydia's tone would have been amusing. "Good God, I must be slipping. Nine times? Really?"

"Really."

"Nine times and you haven't...?" A gesture eliminated the need to complete the question.

"No. We haven't."

"Do you want to?"

Donna darted a brief glance at the condom packet. "It's very complicated."

"Why do I have the feeling that's an understatement?" The question was wry. Lydia leaned forward. "You *have* gotten beyond the he-looks-at-you and you-look-at-him stage, haven't you? Or did I totally misread what was going on between you two at Celebrity Saturday?"

Donna crossed her legs, the memory of a series of tender kisses and tantalizing caresses triggering a quiver of pleasure deep within her. "No, you didn't misread anything," she replied after a moment, her voice huskier than usual. "And yes, we've gotten beyond the looking stage."

"But?"

Donna sighed. She rubbed the nape of her neck with the palm of her right hand. "You know I went to Marty's place at the beach the day after Celebrity Saturday."

"You mentioned it."

"Well, I went there expecting we might..." She pointed to the foil-wrapped packet.

"Uh-huh." Lydia had slipped into her professional mode, encouraging Donna to talk but essentially remaining aloof.

"I'm just about positive he expected the same thing." Donna shifted, remembering the erotic way Marty's compelling gaze had moved over her body as they'd sat in the lambently golden glow of the late afternoon sun. She felt her nipples start to tighten. Her pulse accelerated. He'd wanted her. He'd wanted her as much as she'd wanted him. "But then, oh, I don't know how to explain it, Lydia. One moment Marty was looking at me like it was his birthday and I was the perfect present. The next he was making inane conversation about going into the house to get me a refill."

"A refill?"

"My glass of mineral water was empty."

"Ah."

"Then he said he might have some beer stashed away someplace. He also offered to pop the cork on the champagne Barry Cooperman sent him after that episode outside The Funny Farm. And that's when I, well, one thing led to another and I ended up telling him I'm a recovering alcoholic."

"At which point he backed off," Lydia deduced after several seconds.

"Not exactly."

"Not exactly?"

Donna took a steadying breath. Then, as simply as she could, she related what had—and hadn't—happened on the deck of Marty's beachfront home. Once she started talking, it was difficult to stem the flow of words. She found herself describing the uncertain pattern of her involvement with Marty. The stop-start-stop quality of so many of their conversations. The frustrating mix of desire and denial that permeated the physical side of their relationship. The troubling sense of knowing, yet not knowing.

"I think...Marty's father had a drinking problem," Donna finally said, summing up the conclusions she'd reached after many painful hours of reflection. "I also think Marty was physically abused. Of course, I could be totally wrong. But that's the feeling I've got. In any case, Marty has a lot of secrets."

"Which he isn't willing to share with you." Lydia's dark eyes held a vivid mix of compassion and concern.

"No." Donna's memory flashed back to the exchange she and Marty had had in the Center's parking lot at the end of Celebrity Saturday. "You don't tell things like that," he'd said, ostensibly referring to Sam's refusal to confide the truth about his father. "At least, not intentionally."

"And you haven't pressed him?"

"I've thought about asking him. About trying to get him to talk. I've been on the verge of it more times than I can count. But when things are going well between us, I don't want to risk spoiling them. And when they aren't..." Donna shook her head, knitting her fingers together then unraveling them.

"Are you afraid of him?"

The question rocked Donna to the core. "Of Marty?" she gasped. "God, no, Lydia! Absolutely not. I may be a little afraid *for* him at this point, but never *of* him. Never. Ever."

Lydia contemplated this response for nearly thirty seconds. Then, carefully, "You care about him a lot, don't you?"

Donna closed her eyes for a moment. She faced herself. She faced the truth. Finally she reopened her eyes and faced her friend once again. "It's more than that, Lydia," she admitted simply. "Much more."

"You've considered the emotional baggage he's probably carrying if you're right about his family background?"

"Of course I've considered it! But we both know I'm not exactly walking around empty-handed when it comes to emotional baggage. Even though I've told Marty about my alcoholism, I haven't told him everything. I mean—" Donna swallowed hard "—the way I was when I was drinking—"

"You made mistakes," Lydia interrupted. "Mistakes you've recognized and spent nearly twelve years trying to repair. You've dealt with your past. Not perfectly. Good Lord, you're only human! But you *have* dealt with it. And in the process, you've become one of the strongest, most generous people I've ever known. Now, I think Marty Knight is a special man. A *good* man. And it's obvious that there's a whole lot of chemistry between you two. Still. Please. I want you to remember that a relationship is supposed to have balance. And it can't have balance if one of the people in it does all the giving while the other does all the taking. Or if one of the people opens up while the other stays closed down. You have a right to so much more than a one-way street in life, Donna. I realize you may have trouble accepting that, but you do. You deserve a man who'll be there for you the way you're there for him. You deserve a man who'll love you for your strength and generosity, not just need you for it. And if what you've said about Marty Knight is true..."

Donna Day's head understood what her friend was warning against. Her heart understood the warning came too late.

Marty Knight might not be the man she *deserved*, but he was the man she'd fallen in love with.

Eight

In a room crammed with some of the most glamorous females Hollywood had to offer, there was only one woman Marty Knight wanted to watch. Donna Day drew his gaze the way a magnet draws iron.

They'd arrived at Arnold Golding's Beverly Hills mansion about ninety minutes before. Marty had felt protective of Donna when they'd walked in. He'd long since learned that to go with the flow at one of Arnold's bashes was to swim with sharks and piranhas. Because his "affair" with Donna had been featured in just about every tabloid on the stands during the past seven days—Day For Knight, Knight And Day: Is She the One?, Together: Knight And Day, and Will Day Become Knight? were just some of the headlines—he'd been concerned that she might become the target of one or more pairs of perfectly capped teeth.

He needn't have worried. It had quickly become evident that Donnie Day's daughter knew how to handle the Tinsel Town social scene.

They'd separated after about a half hour. She'd been waylaid by an old friend of her father's. He'd been annexed by Arnold Golding and taken off to meet someone named Melon.

"Melon?" Marty had repeated carefully.

"Yeah," the executive producer had affirmed. "Her real name is Mary Ellen but everyone calls her Melon. And no jokes about casabas or cantaloupes, okay? She's—achoo! —sensitive."

"Okay. I won't say anything about honeydews, either. Speaking of which, what happened to Dixie?"

"Who?"

"Weren't you dating a former Miss Peach Fuzz named Dixie?"

"Oh." A sniffle. "Yeah." A second sniffle. "Her." A third sniffle. "We broke up. She started aggravating my allergies."

"I gather, ah, Melon's doing her best to soothe them?"

"Well—" Arnold had sneezed violently at this point, which Marty had sensed did not bode well for Melon's longevity. "Let's just say I woke up with clear sinuses this morning."

Melon had turned out to be blond, blue-eyed and buxom. Marty had squandered a few minutes plumbing the shallows of her personality and trying not to grit his teeth at her high-pitched giggle. Arnold had been in the middle of a sneezing attack when he'd finally managed to extricate himself.

He'd mingled a bit after that, then settled himself in a spot where he could keep an eye on Donna. She was standing on the opposite side of the guest-thronged room, talking with the director who'd taken the top prize at the Cannes Film Festival a few weeks before. Although the man was reputed to be inarticulate to the point of speaking exclusively in monosyllables, he was babbling like a brook in response to Donna's encouraging smile.

Well, maybe it wasn't *just* her smile . . .

"She is lovely," Marty murmured to himself. He took a drink from the glass of ginger ale he was holding.

Start with her glossy red-brown hair. Her smooth, face-framing bob made a mockery of most of the other coiffures in the room. Where those pseudo artless styles had probably taken hours to arrange, hers had been achieved with a few licks of a brush. A man knew, instinctively, that touching Donna's hair would be like touching strands of freshly washed silk. There'd be no feel of gel or mousse or industrial strength fixative.

Move on to her makeup. She was wearing a bit more than usual, but the impression it created was one of subtle enhancement rather than artifice. Her eyes glowed, jewel-like, in their lush frame of darkened lashes. Her rose-tinted mouth illustrated the meaning of the word provocative.

And then there was her dress.

It was black and it was basic.

The design was off-the-shoulder and austerely simple. The garment hinted at the sleek curves beneath, but didn't hug them. And, like a perfectly crafted sentence, it was long enough to cover the subject yet short enough to be interesting.

Very interesting.

Marty stiffened suddenly. His fingers tightened on his glass as he watched Donna start fluffing her hair with her left hand. The act of raising her arm caused the trio of crystal and onyx bracelets she was wearing to slide about halfway to her elbow. It also caused the hem of her dress to slide about halfway up her thighs.

Maybe a little *too* interesting.

Donna finished fluffing. She lowered her arm. The bracelets settled back around her slender wrist. The bottom edge of her dress returned to a relatively demure position, an inch or so above her knees.

The stiffness eased out of most—but not all—of Marty's body.

He wanted her. He wanted her so badly he ached. And she wanted him in return. Every time he touched her she went up like tinder. She was his for the asking.

So why in hell am I holding back? he asked himself, downing another gulp of ginger ale.

You know damned well why, came his uncompromising reply.

Yeah. He did. And it got down to a very basic truth.

He was holding back because deep in his gut he realized that a woman like Donna Elizabeth Day deserved—

"Much better than you, ol' buddy."

The slightly slurred statement came from someone standing to Marty's left. He knew the identity of that someone even before he turned to face the shaggy-haired man who'd spoken.

The man was a comic who'd been christened John Thomas Newsom. He was known as J.T. He had never been, nor would he ever be, one of Marty's friends. He was an acquaintance. A fellow traveler on the comedy club circuit. An occasional rival, in years gone by, for gigs and girls.

He'd also been an eyewitness to one of the worst moments of Marty's life.

"Tonight you'll talk to me, huh?" J.T. was holding a glass of vodka in his right hand. He gestured with the glass, then knocked back a slug of the liquor it contained.

"When have I not talked to you?" Marty countered, controlling both his face and voice. J.T. wasn't drunk, but he was definitely working on it. He'd been working on it the first time they'd met, too.

"*When?*" J.T. leaned in slightly. He peered at Marty with bloodshot eyes. "Try maybe three weeks ago. At Zeke's place. You blew me off like I was a bunch of dead leaves, man."

It took Marty a moment to figure out what J.T. was referring to.

Oh...yes. At The Funny Farm. The night he'd met Donna. J.T. had come up to him at the bar after the autograph seekers and before Barry Cooperman. And he had, indeed, brushed the guy off like lint.

"Is it all coming back to you?" J.T. inquired.

"Yeah," Marty answered, forking a hand through his hair. "Look, I'm sorry if I was rude."

"You were. But I found other company." J.T. chuckled with a hint of malice. "I read about the slugfest between you and that dipstick Barry Cooperman in one of those supermarket rags. God, I love tabloids! I get some of my best material out of them. Anyway, I feel bad about missing it. The fight, I mean. Would've been like old times, huh?"

Marty's stomach knotted. "No," he denied flatly. "Not at all."

"Oh, come on, Marty. I heard you really knocked the crap out of the guy. 'Course it only took you—what?—two, maybe three, punches to put your old—"

"Leave it alone, J.T.," Marty interrupted. The words came out a lot more sharply than he'd intended.

J.T. cocked a brow. "Why?"

Marty waited a beat, mentally hammering the edge off his voice. "Because it happened ten years ago," he replied, feigning a cool he didn't feel. "And nostalgia isn't what it used to be."

J.T. took another drink while he considered this. "Okay. Sure," he finally said, then turned his head. "She's nice," he said, nodding in Donna's direction. "Very nice."

The knot in Marty's stomach tightened. He glanced across the room. A notoriously lecherous film reviewer had just oozed up next to the Cannes prizewinner. The man was eyeing Donna as though she was the ultimate in coming attractions. He sidled closer to her. Donna seemed oblivious to both his ogling and his encroachment.

If that son of a bitch so much as *breathes* on her wrong... Marty left the thought unfinished.

"Yes," he said tersely. "She is nice."

"Well, I can certainly see what you see in her," J.T. commented. He sipped from his glass again. "The question is, what does she see in you? Like I said when I walked up—"

Marty stopped him with a look. Just a look. "I heard what you said when you walked up, man."

The other comic made a placating gesture. "Chill out, dude. Geez. Give a guy a series and he starts taking himself so-o-o-o-o seriously."

Marty took a deep breath, trying to center and steady himself. He had a bad feeling. A bad, bad feeling. As if the walls were closing in or the ceiling was coming down. As if a storm was about to break.

As if his past was about to catch up with him...

He realized he'd clenched the fingers of his free hand into a fist. He forced himself to pry them open. He glanced to-

ward Donna once again. Something had happened while he
hadn't been watching. Whatever it had been, it had caused
the reviewer to beat a hasty retreat. Donna was nodding at
the filmmaker from Cannes, her expression serene.

Suddenly, almost as if she felt the touch of his gaze, she
turned her head in Marty's direction. The crystal earrings
that dangled from her earlobes swayed with the movement.

Green eyes met brown.

Donna smiled.

What the eye contact hadn't done to scramble Marty's
body and brain, the slow, sweet curving of Donna's lips
pretty much took care of.

The plushly carpeted floor seemed to tilt. The tempera-
ture in the room soared by at least five degrees. The air
quivered with electricity, as if it had been charged by a
lightning strike.

After a few moments, Marty became dimly aware that
J.T. was speaking to him. It was hard to make sense of the
words through the sledgehammer pounding of his pulse.

"Wh-what?" he asked, hauling his gaze back to the other
comic. He suspected he was grinning like a loon. He managed to drag some air into his lungs. The process wasn't
easy, but it was preferable to acute oxygen deprivation.

"Look, man, I know it's probably no big deal to you,"
J.T. said sarcastically. He finished off the liquor in his glass.
"You, Mr. Hot Shot, who got points off the gross *and* his
name above the title in his first feature film. But I figure this
part could get me noticed, you know? So what if the director's a certified nut case, the leading lady's the producer's
latest bimbo and the location is Hicksville, Ohio? This picture could be huge. Kind of a cross between *Lethal Weapon*
and *Field of Dreams* with a little bit of *Animal House*
thrown in. And I get featured billing."

"Sounds great," Marty responded, hoping he sounded
sincere. "Congratulations."

"Screw congratulations." J.T. snagged Marty's arm.
"Have a drink with me."

Marty pulled free of the other man's grasp. The bad feeling he'd had a few minutes before was back and it was worse

than ever. He lifted the glass he was still holding. "I've got a drink," he said, rattling the half-melted ice cubes.

"Yeah, what! Ginger ale?"

"Look—"

J.T.'s expression turned ugly. "You're scared, aren't you?"

Marty's breath sawed in and out. He knew the kind of ugliness he was seeing in the other man's eyes. He'd gotten intimately acquainted with it at an early age.

"Of you?" he countered. His voice was as steady as a diamond cutter's hand.

J.T. shook his head, his straw-colored hair flopping untidily around his face. "No. Of *you.* I wondered about you from the start, man. The no-dope line, I could buy. You didn't need to get chicks stoned to score with them. And anybody could see you got a better high from doing stand-up than you'd ever get from sniffing snow. But the no-drinking angle, that I wondered about. To say nothing of wondering about the expression you'd get whenever I got sloshed in your company. I mean, you'd look at me like I was too low to bother puking on."

"J.T.—"

"And then I met your old man and I understood. I understood—"

"Shut up."

Another shake of the head. J.T.'s eyes were cold and uncaring. "Deep down you're scared you're just like him, aren't you, Marty? A loser. An abuser. A ready-made boozer. It felt good to hit him that night, didn't it? It felt good to pay him back for all the—"

"Shut up!"

A third head shake. J.T.'s voice got louder. "You figure you're safe as long as you don't drink. You figure all that fear will stay locked away like some dirty little secret. You figure nobody'll ever know about you and your old man. Well, I've got a news flash for you, man—"

Marty dropped the glass he was holding and turned away. He didn't want to hear.

God help him, he didn't *need* to hear. There was nothing John Thomas Newsom could say on this subject that he hadn't already said himself.

But he did hear. And so, he knew with a sickening sense of shame, did Donna. He'd caught sight of her as he'd pivoted, searching for an escape route. She'd been standing, stricken, a little more than a yard away.

"—Like father, like son," J.T. said.

Marty knew he had to get out.
He did.
Donna knew she had to follow him.
She did.

Donna finally caught up with Marty about halfway down the long, curving drive that led to Arnold Golding's palatial home. She might not have caught up with him at all if he hadn't come to a sudden halt after the fifth time she'd called his name.

She approached him warily, the way she might approach a wild, wounded animal. She was not afraid for herself but for him.

What if she said the wrong thing?

What if she did the wrong thing?

When she thought of the compassion he'd shown Sam Collins and the other children at the Center...

When she thought of the tenderness he'd shown her...

Yes, Marty Knight was laden with emotional baggage. But, dear heaven, he'd found a way to carry it with incredible grace.

She loved him. For better or worse, she loved him. And she could only hope that her love would be enough to help ease his pain.

"Marty?" she asked softly, moving up behind him. It was a cloudless night. Although the moon was on the wane, it shed enough illumination so she didn't have to strain to see the outline of his motionless body. His head was bent. His shoulders were braced. His hands were fisted at his sides.

Right foot.
Left foot.

Right foot.

The *click* of her high-heeled evening sandals against the asphalt drive seemed unnervingly loud to Donna. So did the hammering of her heart.

Left foot.

Right foot.

Left foot.

Close enough to extend her arm and touch him.

She stopped, clasping her hands together. It was not the time to touch. Not . . . yet.

"Marty?" she repeated.

He pivoted to face her. Wordlessly. Without warning.

It wasn't the abruptness of his movement that made Donna take a stumbling step backward. It was the anguish she saw in his expression when he turned around. She caught her breath sharply, feeling herself pale.

Marty misread her reaction. He froze, his body going rigid. Anguish turned to agony, which turned to something even worse.

"Dear God," he said. His voice was shaking. He looked absolutely shattered. "You thought I was going to hit you."

"No," Donna denied, appalled. She shook her head back and forth. The dangling earrings she was wearing swung wildly, buffeting her bloodless cheeks.

"You did."

"No!"

Marty may as well have been deaf for all the weight he gave to her words, blind for all the attention he paid to her presence. He lifted his hands, palms up, fingers splayed. He stared down at them for several moments then said tautly, "I swear, I would cut these off before I ever, ever hurt . . ."

Donna couldn't stand it. She took two steps forward and clasped his hands with hers. Palms kissed palms. Fingers twined like lovers. "I know that, Marty," she told him with passionate conviction. "I know that."

His grasp tightened convulsively, as though her touch had triggered a response within him he couldn't control. Then, with a half-swallowed sound that could have been the first syllable of her name, Marty yanked his hands free of hers.

"How can you know?" he demanded harshly. "You saw me that night. In the alley. Outside The Funny Farm. You saw me with Barry Cooperman! You saw how I—"

"I saw you were trying to protect me, Marty! I also saw that you let—you *let*—Barry Cooperman hurt you more than you ever tried to hurt him." Donna swallowed, picking her next words very deliberately. "You're not a violent person, Marty. You are *not* an abuser."

There was a long silence. Donna watched Marty's eyes flick back and forth, back and forth. She met his searching gaze steadily, trying to communicate how deep her trust in him ran.

"You...heard," he said finally, clearly referring to the exchange that had precipitated his exit from the party.

"Some."

Marty drew a shuddery breath, then expelled it on a hissing sigh. He averted his head. "So you know." His tone was bleak.

"No," she disputed gently, watching his profile. "I don't. But I want to. Why don't you tell me?"

Another shuddery inhalation. Another hissing sigh. His jaw clenched and unclenched.

"My father drank," he finally admitted, clearly struggling to get the words out. "Not all the time. I mean, he'd go weeks, sometimes months, without touching a drop. And then..." He shook his head.

There was no pretty way to put it. Even if there had been, Donna would have opted for directness.

"He'd get drunk and he'd hit you," she said without inflection.

"He didn't mean it."

Marty's response was obviously reflexive. An excuse offered lord knew how many times before. Donna had to bite the inside of her cheek to keep from protesting it.

Marty turned his eyes back to hers for a few moments. "It wasn't always bad, Donna. There were times when he was a good guy. A good dad. Times when he was..." His throat worked suddenly and he looked away from her again. "He broke my collarbone when I was eleven. I think the worst was afterward. When he sobered up and saw what had happened, what he'd done. He cried. My father cried right there in front of me. And then he told me I was his boy and he loved me and it would never happen again.''

Donna squeezed her eyelids shut for a split second. ''But it did,'' she asserted after she reopened them.

Marty's lips twisted. ''Actually, no. He only broke my collarbone once.''

He gave the contradiction an almost joking inflection. The sound of it made Donna want to cry. ''Marty—''

''I left home right after I graduated from high school.'' He went on as though she hadn't spoken, as though it were perfectly natural to gloss over seven years of his life. Donna watched him lift his right hand to that chain that hung around his neck. She didn't have to ask who'd inspired him to hang in long enough to get his diploma. ''I had to cut the cord. I kicked around. I did a lot of minimum-wage jobs before I finally got a toehold on the low end of the comedy food chain. That's where I met...'' He inclined his head back toward Arnold Golding's mansion.

''J.T. Newsom,'' Donna said, unable to hide her distaste. She knew the identity of the man who'd sent Marty out into the night because she'd seen him on television several times.

''Yeah,'' Marty affirmed, glancing at her once again. ''We were on the circuit together. We weren't friends. But we shared a lot of bookings. And one night—the night I turned twenty-one as a matter of fact—we shared a booking in a dive on the south side of Chicago.''

He stopped, turning his head. His gaze seemed to fix on something out in the darkness. Donna waited. And waited. Finally he went on.

''It was late. I was the closing act. J.T. was sitting at the bar. I was a couple of jokes into my act when this... drunk...started heckling me. I gave it right back to him, but he wouldn't quit. He kept heckling. And heckling. And then he said something and I suddenly realized that this heckler...this *drunk* ...was my father.''

Donna sank her teeth into her lower lip. A moment later she tasted the coppery tang of her own blood.

"Something inside me snapped," Marty continued, his voice turning rough. "I came down off the stage and I—I went for him." He brought his left hand up, fingers contracting into a fist. "I got him by the front of his shirt and I nailed him. *Bam.*" He spat out the word. "And then I nailed him again. *Bam.*"

He paused. Slowly, ever so slowly, he opened his clenched fingers. Slowly, he lowered his hand. His movements had a ritualistic quality to them.

When he resumed speaking, his voice was as flat and colorless as a pane of glass.

"And then I let go of his shirt and I walked away. I heard later somebody found a number in his wallet and phoned my mother to take him home. I don't know. I was long gone by the time she showed up. But that was the last time ever I saw my father. He died of a heart attack a few years later."

Donna's eyes stung. Her throat ached. Her chest felt as if it had been banded with steel straps. "Oh, Marty," she whispered. "I'm so sorry."

His eyes slewed toward her face. He looked at her as if the words she'd just uttered made no sense at all to him.

"Why should you say that?" he asked, shaking his head. "*You* didn't do anything wrong."

She heard the guilt in his voice. Saw the shame in his eyes. Knew the self-inflicted pain he was struggling to endure.

"Dear God, Marty," she said shakily, reaching out to him. "Neither did you."

For one terrible moment Donna thought he was going to reject her words, and her. Then, with a suddenness that made her head spin, she was in his arms. He was holding her. Hugging her. Invoking her name over and over again in a husky voice.

"Donna, Donna, Donna."

"Marty—"

She turned her face up to his. He brushed his mouth over her brow, her eyelashes and her cheeks before finally claiming her lips. She opened to him without hesitation. He drank in her sweetness with a throttled groan.

"Come home with me tonight, Donna," he urged. His body moved against her, wordlessly communicating the strength of his hunger. He kissed one corner of her mouth and then the other, charting the ripe curve between with the tip of his tongue. "Stay with me. Make love with me."

Donna pulled back, just a little. Even as she did so, her fingers slid up the front of his shirt. She relished the muscular resilience she felt beneath the fine cotton fabric.

"Please." The word came rumbling up from deep inside his chest. His dark eyes burned into hers. "I need you."

Donna trembled.

And I *love* you, she thought.

"Please," Marty said again. His long-fingered hands moved up her back with exquisite gentleness. His caress was not that of a man who intended to take without giving in return.

Donna trembled again. Then, with a full understanding of what she was about to do, she offered the man she loved the answer he needed.

"Yes."

Nine

The possibility that Donna's "yes" could become a "no" gnawed at Marty every instant of their drive back to his beach house. Nothing—not the promise in her smile, not the passion in her eyes, not even the provocative stroke of her fingers against his taut upper thigh—could blunt the bite of uncertainty.

Until she was in his arms...

Until she'd taken him into her body...

Until they lay together afterward, still joined in the most intimate way imaginable...

Nothing between them was inevitable, he warned himself over and over. Nothing was preordained.

Yet as braced as Marty was for rejection, the tiny hesitation he detected in Donna's fluid stride as they neared his front door still hit him with the force of a physical blow. He almost cried out. He'd learned many years before that crying out against pain didn't help.

"You've changed your mind," he said, his voice deep, his breathing disciplined.

Donna looked up at him, eyes wide, lips slightly parted. "No," she denied throatily.

"Second thoughts?"

She flushed. The moon's silvery light leeched most of the color out of her face. The sudden rush of blood to her cheeks was very obvious.

"*A* ... thought," she amended.

Marty was close enough to smell the wildflower scent of her perfume. He allowed himself to inhale it deeply.

He was close enough to feel the shimmering warmth of her flesh, too. He allowed himself to luxuriate in its living heat, as well.

He was also close enough to touch her. But that, he did not let himself do. Not yet.

"What kind of thought?"

Donna angled her chin upward. The crystal earrings she was wearing swayed gently. Her gaze captured his. The expression in her deep green eyes did a good job of undermining the dwindling stability of his knees. Whatever her thought was, it definitely didn't involve the word no.

"The thought that we're both adults," she answered. "The thought that we've both lived adult lives before tonight."

Understanding came abruptly. And in its wake came a dizzying sense of relief. "You want me to use a condom," he said bluntly.

Donna nodded. Her flush intensified. "If you don't have—"

"I do," he assured her. He'd purchased the means to protect her two weeks ago, after she'd accepted his invitation to spend a day at the beach. Lifting his hands, he cupped Donna's face. "I want it to be you and me tonight," he told her. "No past. Only present. Just the two of us. Alone. Together. Making love. I'll keep you safe, Donna. *I promise.*"

The first thing he did was kiss her. Lowering his head, he cherished her mouth with his own. Nibbling. Nuzzling. Claiming. Caressing.

He licked her lips with quick, catlike strokes that made her breath quicken and her body quiver. She opened to him with a murmurous sound of approval, her eyelids fluttering down as her arms flowed up to clasp his broad shoulders. The movements of his tongue turned sinuous. She shifted against him, her restless movements offering both provocation and pleasure.

"Yes," he whispered, savoring the sweet tastes and satiny textures that were erotically familiar in some ways, erotically fresh in others. He caught Donna's lower lip between his teeth, biting down with exquisitely calibrated care. He felt a shudder run through her and heard her say his name on a ragged breath.

Her hands spasmed on his shoulders. Her slender fingers dug into him with surprising strength.

"Yes," she sighed.

She sighed again when Marty finally lifted his mouth from hers. He smiled down at her, cataloguing the many signals that her hunger was keeping pace with his. There would be no rushing this consummation. When he had spoken of the two of them, together, he'd meant together—all the way.

Donna matched Marty's smile with one of her own. She tilted her head back, the muscles of her neck as pliant as sun-warmed wax. She felt a subtle tug on her earlobes as her earrings shifted. The idea of wearing earrings at a time like this suddenly struck her as absurd. She lifted her hands to pull them off.

"No," Marty said huskily, divining her intention and forestalling it by the simple expedient of capturing her wrists. "Let me do it."

"All r-right," Donna acquiesced, her voice catching in her throat. She lowered her arms.

Donna had never known, never suspected, that the simple act of having her earrings removed by a man could make her tremble to the very center of her soul.

He stroked the left side of her jaw with the knuckles of his right hand, urging her to turn her head. She did. He brushed her hair back, straining the silken strands between his fingers. A voluptuous growl of approbation eased out of him.

He charted the outer rim of her ear, then teased his finger inward. His touch triggered a tingling sensation that arrowed clear down to Donna's prettily pedicured toes. She swayed.

Marty slipped off her left earring and let it drop to the floor. He massaged her earlobe with his thumb and forefinger for several seconds.

Donna closed her eyes. She opened them on a gasp a moment later when she felt the fan of Marty's breath against her cheek followed by the delicate nip of his teeth against her ear.

"That's one," he informed her in velvety whisper, then brushed a kiss against the hollow where her pulse beat.

It was at least a minute—maybe two, maybe three—before Donna heard him whisper, "That's two." What happened in the interim left her clinging to him for support.

"Marty..."

He kissed her again. The claim of his mouth was deeper this time. More devouring. Donna kissed him back hungrily. She arched her body, wanting to get closer to him. Marty stroked his hands up from her slender waist to her bare, silken-skinned shoulders. Reversing direction, he kneaded his way down her spine, defining each feminine curve, holding her hard against the thrust of his rising masculinity.

"Let me," she insisted unevenly a short time later, peeling his jacket off his shoulders and down his arms. She discarded the garment carelessly, then began to undo the buttons on the front of his shirt.

Marty let Donna have her way with him, to a point. There was something incredibly arousing about the intensity she brought to the task she'd set for herself.

One button.

Two.

Three.

Four...

His shirt was followed, very shortly, by Donna's basic black dress.

The sequence in which their remaining garments were shed—who did what for whom and in what order—was never very clear to Marty. The actions that took them from semi-nudity to nakedness to sensual abandonment on his bed were lost in a white-hot blur.

There was no uncertainty between them. Their awareness of each other was absolute, their attunement total. What might have been an awkward interruption—the few moments Marty needed to fulfill his promise of protection—became a bone-melting affirmation of mutual trust and tenderness.

To touch...

To taste...

Donna stroked Marty's bare torso with both hands, playing with the springy crispness of his chest hair and the sleekly muscled power of the flesh beneath. Her lips curved upward in a tiny smile of satisfaction as her fingertips found the dark rosettes of his male nipples. She traced them delicately, relishing her lover-to-be's groan of response as she teased the twin nubbins of sensitive flesh to hardness.

He groaned again when she dipped her head and lapped at one nipple, then kissed her way across his chest to sample the flavor of the other.

"Donna..."

She lifted her head, cheeks flushed, eyes fever bright, and smiled at him.

Marty shifted himself, then her. He caressed her body with his hands, gleaning more and more of her womanly secrets as he fed the passionate fires he had ignited. He cupped her rose-tipped breasts gently, discovering that their lovely shape fit his palms even more perfectly than he had imagined nearly two weeks earlier.

Donna whimpered when Marty claimed the peak of her right breast with his lips. He lapped at her with his tongue, then took her deep into his hot, hungry mouth. The tug on her nipple provoked a sudden contraction deep within her body. He sucked again. A cry of pleasure broke from her lips.

He took possession of her other nipple, raking the very peak of it with the serrated edge of his front teeth. She arched up. He drew her in.

"Marty, oh, please..."

Much as she'd done only minutes before, he lifted his head and smiled.

A few seconds later she felt his fingers brush against the cluster of auburn curls that sheltered the core of her femininity. She shifted, opening to him, trembling in anticipation.

He touched her. Delicately at first, then more and more deeply. Donna twisted in counterpoint to his intimate caresses, conscious of the primitive sensual pressures building within her. A series of tiny shudders racked her.

Their lips met in a searing kiss. Tongues mated. Breaths married.

"Want you..."

"Y-yes."

"Need you..."

"Yes."

"Donna..."

"Now, Marty..."

He joined them, sliding into the center of her liquid heat. Her hips rose up to meet his thrust, deepening his possession at the same time she asserted hers.

There was no holding back. No hesitation. He moved, slowly at first, then more and more swiftly. She moved with him. Willingly. Wildly. He groaned, feeling the first rippling spasms that signaled she was on the brink of release. A moment later he was on the edge of ecstasy, as well.

Donna clung to Marty. Needing him. Wanting him. Loving him. She shuddered again and again before finally shattering in response to a pleasure so intense there was no resisting it or the man who was giving it to her.

"Marty!" she cried out.

At that instant Marty Knight learned there was one sound in the world that could stir him even more potently than the sound of Donna Day's laughter.

An instant later he was beyond learning anything. He could only feel. And what he felt was like nothing he'd ever experienced in his life.

Afterward, they slept.

They stirred awake, together, many hours later. He

reached for her. She reached for him. They reached for what they'd had before and they found it.

Afterward, they slept again.

When Donna stirred awake for the second time, shortly after dawn, she was alone.

She found Marty outside on the deck.

He was leaning on the railing, staring out at the ocean. His only item of clothing was a well-worn pair of jeans.

There were several scratch marks on the upper part of his tanned, smoothly muscled back. The realization that she was responsible for putting them there gave Donna a jolt. It also sent a surge of hot blood rushing up into her cheeks.

She studied Marty in silence for nearly a minute, trying to gauge his mood, trying to guess what had prompted him to leave his bed . . . and her.

It would be a long time before she forgot the awful jumble of emotions she'd experienced in the first few moments after she'd woken up and discovered she was naked in a bed that wasn't hers in a room she couldn't remember ever having seen. She'd felt shock. Panic. Confusion. Shame. She'd felt herself cartwheeling back to the past. Demons she'd spent years casting out suddenly started hissing that they hadn't been exorcised after all . . . they'd been in hiding.

Then, mercifully, her brain had started to function and she'd realized where she was and how she'd gotten there. The shock had eased, the panic subsided. The confusion and the shame had drained away.

Her pulse rate had slowed and her breathing pattern had smoothed out.

It's all right, she'd told herself. This is Marty's bed. Marty's room. And what I did with Marty—in this room, in this bed—I did because I love him.

She'd sat up, instinctively clutching the bed sheet against her body. She'd remained in that position for several seconds, listening for some indication of Marty's whereabouts.

The whoosh of a shower.

The flush of a toilet.

The rattle of pots and pans.

She'd strained to detect any of these sounds. She'd heard nothing but the crash of waves breaking on the beach.

She'd said Marty's name aloud at that point, her voice holding a blend of yearning and uneasiness. There'd been no answer.

She'd waited a few more seconds, then thrust aside the sheets and gotten out of bed. She'd been conscious of an unfamiliar tenderness in her breasts and a faintly pleasurable throb between her thighs. Memories of the night before had set off a series of rippling tremors deep inside her, like the aftershocks of a great earthquake.

She'd said Marty's name a second time, raising her voice slightly as she'd done so. Again, there'd been no answer.

She'd glanced around the room, feeling herself flush as she inventoried the two sets of clothing strewn on the bleached wood floor. The vividness of her memories had increased.

Her gaze had eventually settled on the white cotton shirt Marty had been wearing the night before. She'd crossed the room to the discarded garment and picked it up. Her nostrils had quivered for an instant as she'd caught Marty's musky male scent. After a brief hesitation, she'd slipped the shirt on and fastened about half the buttons. Then she'd shoved up the sleeves and gone in search of her lover.

Well, she'd found him. The question was: What did she do now that she had?

A sudden breeze sent a lock of hair unfurling across Donna's face like a ribbon. She brushed it away with an impatient wipe of her fingers. She was conscious that her heart had gone into overdrive. She shifted her weight from one bare foot to the other, moistening her suddenly dry lips with a lick of her tongue. Squaring her shoulders, she drew a steadying breath and prepared to say Marty's name for the third time since she'd awakened. She was determined that this time, there would be an answer.

Her mouth opened.

Before she spoke, Marty pivoted around.

He'd sensed Donna's presence nearly a minute before. The knowledge that she was awake and near suffused him with a rare kind of warmth. Still, he had not turned to face her right away. He'd had to gather his courage first.

The *before* with Donna had been hard yet liberating in ways he was just beginning to grasp. The *during* had been the most extraordinary experience of his life. But now the moment had arrived when he must deal with the *after*...

He let his dark-eyed gaze wash over her like a wave, sluicing from the top of her sleep-ruffled hair to the tips of her pink-lacquered toenails. While he'd never been especially turned on by the notion of women wearing men's clothing, the realization that Donna had on his shirt and nothing else affected him like an intimate caress. The hunger he'd leashed so firmly when he'd surfaced from slumber roughly an hour earlier stirred, stretched and began to prowl.

"Hi," he said finally, his voice huskier than normal.

Donna responded in kind, a tentative smile flickering around the corners of her lips. After a moment she walked out onto the deck. Each step she took offered Marty an enticing flash of thigh. He could see the subtle movement of her breasts beneath the white cotton of his shirt, as well.

She came to a halt about two yards away from him. She gestured back toward the house. "I, uh, woke up and...and you weren't there."

Not for lack of wanting to be, he thought frankly. He'd been fully aroused when he'd awakened. It had taken every ounce of discipline he had not to succumb to his desire...and to Donna.

The kitten-soft fan of her breath across his chest.

The tease of her silken hair beneath his chin.

The press of her naked breasts against—

Marty adjusted his position abruptly and cleared his throat. "I thought you might need some rest," he answered. His reply was the truth, but far from the whole truth.

"Oh." Color blossomed in Donna's cheeks as she absorbed the implications of this. "Well..."

"I also needed a little time by myself to sort some things out."

Donna had felt herself blush, now she felt herself pale. "What kind of things did you need to sort out, Marty?" she asked carefully, tilting her chin.

He waited for a moment, then held out his right hand to her. It was steady. So was his gaze. After a fractional hesitation, Donna walked forward and took what was being offered. Her fingers interlaced with his.

There was a short silence.

"What kind of things?" she eventually repeated.

Marty rubbed the palm of his free hand against his left thigh, clearly uneasy. "I'm afraid I haven't had a lot of experience with morning-after-the-night-before etiquette," he said obliquely. He glanced away from her. "As a matter of fact, I don't have any experience at all."

"I—I don't understand."

Marty took a deep breath, then swung his eyes back to meet hers. "I've never slept with a woman before, Donna," he informed her bluntly. "Had sex with, yes. But I've never made love with a woman and then gone to sleep with her in my arms."

Donna's heart turned over in her breast as she realized what he was admitting. "Oh," she managed to say.

"And you're the first woman I've ever . . . had . . . here."

"Oh," she said again.

"So, when I woke up with you this morning—" his hand tightened around hers for an instant "—I didn't, I mean, well, let's just say, it's . . . it's going to take some getting used to."

"*It?*" Donna was trembling on the verge of something wonderful. But she wouldn't—couldn't—let herself define what that something might be.

"You and me. Last night."

She caught her breath.

Marty knew his answer had disappointed her. He also knew he could go no further, say no more. At least not yet. Like a toddler trying to learn how to walk, he was off-balance and uncertain. There was an odd exhilaration in this, to be sure. But there was also an awareness that one wrong step could send him tumbling. He had no doubts about his ability to endure a fall. What he feared was the possibility of taking Donna down with him.

Shifting his body, Marty drew Donna closer to him, bringing her to stand between his thighs. She examined him with guarded green eyes. But behind the wariness there was the womanly warmth that had captivated him as surely as her laughter.

. He made a show of inspecting her attire. "You know," he commented, "you do a lot more for that shirt than I ever did."

"You think so?" Donna countered after a few moments, accepting his conversational gambit.

"Oh, yes," he affirmed. He clasped her right hand with his left. "Definitely."

"Mmm." She appeared to consider this. "And just what, exactly, do I do for it?"

He smiled, letting his gaze rove over her. He stroked the fragile skin of her inner wrists with the pads of his thumbs, savoring the unmistakable quickening of her pulse. A sudden puff of wind molded the fabric of his shirt to her slender body. Her taut-tipped breasts were clearly outlined for several heady seconds.

Marty cocked a brow. "There're so many things. It's difficult to know where to begin."

"Try." Donna insinuated herself an inch or two closer to him.

He raised her right hand to his lips and brushed a kiss against her knuckles. Then he turned her hand over and touched his mouth to one of the pulse points he had caressed just a few moments before.

"M-Marty—"

"I'm thinking," he replied, tasting her skin with a swift lick of his tongue. He smiled inwardly as he heard her catch her breath. Deliberately, he turned his attention to her left hand.

First, the knuckles.

He saluted them with a teasing nibble as well as a nuzzling kiss.

Then, the inner wrist, with its translucently fair skin, its delicate tracery of veins and its—

He froze.

. . . before I finally hit bottom.

Two weeks after he'd heard Donna Day say those five words, Marty Knight finally knew how to interpret them. Three whitened scars were the keys to his comprehension.

He looked at the woman whose laughter and lovemaking had taught him more about the beauty of life than he'd ever believed himself capable of learning. He felt her try to withdraw her hand from his. He didn't let her.

"Donna?" he questioned after a jagged moment of silence.

Donna gazed at the man to whom she'd given her heart, unasked and perhaps unwanted. She read no revulsion in his eyes, no condemnatory judgments. What she saw was compassion and caring and concern. And anger. Not anger directed at her, she realized. But anger directed at whatever—or whomever—had driven her to attempt the ultimate act of self-destruction.

"I call them my rebirth marks," she said simply, steadily.

"Rebirth marks?"

"I was one person before. I was a new person after."

Marty traced one of the scars with a feather-light touch. "You usually wear bracelets on your left arm," he said in an odd tone. There was an implied question in the observation.

Donna hesitated. Then, speaking slowly, "I try not to rub my past in people's faces. In the beginning, the bracelets were meant to hide the scars. I'm not proud of them. But now, after so many years, the bracelets are more habit than anything else."

There was a long pause. Finally, Marty spoke.

"Can you—" his features revealed an inner struggle "—*will* you tell me what happened, Donna? Please? I want to know."

It was time for the truth. The whole truth. And nothing but the truth.

Donna drew a cleansing breath, then began to speak.

"I told you my mother died when I was nine. What I didn't tell you is that she died of an overdose of sleeping pills and liquor. Whether it was intentional or an accident, nobody knows. There was no note. But she was a very unhappy person, and my father, as he'd be the first to admit, didn't do much to try to change that. I was away at school when it happened."

"Your parents sent you away to school when you were *nine* years old?"

"Don't fault them, Marty," Donna urged quietly. "I don't know that my childhood would have been any different—any better—if they hadn't. In any case, all I was told was that my mother had suddenly gotten sick and died. Donnie...Donnie didn't handle it very well. I realize now he was suffering from a lot of guilt. The fact that I'd inherited my mother's looks didn't help the situation. But the net result was that I ended up feeling doubly deserted. Doubly rejected."

"And that led you to start drinking when you were thirteen?"

"In a way. I took my first drink the day I found out the truth about my mother's death. A girl I knew showed me a copy of a scandal magazine. You know, the kind that specializes in dragging other people's dirty linen through the mud and then hanging it on a clothesline for everyone to see? Well, this particular magazine had a story about my mother's overdose. It all but said it had been a suicide."

"Oh, Donna."

"I discovered that day that liquor could numb a lot of things I didn't want to feel. It also seemed to fill up the empty places in my life. So, I kept drinking. I never thought it was a problem. I mean, I knew kids who abused alcohol. Or drugs. But I told myself I wasn't like them. I got good grades. Everybody—and I do mean everybody—thought I was such a nice girl. I wasn't any trouble to anyone. Except myself."

"What about the car accident? Dear Lord, Donna, didn't somebody—"

"I told you," she interrupted. "I lied through my teeth about that." She grimaced, shaking her head at the memory. She'd been a practiced deceiver by the time she'd reached sixteen. "Donnie was in Vegas when it happened.

His manager got stuck with the job of smoothing things over. Donnie called me the next day and chewed me out. That done, he pretty much laughed the whole thing off. He even bought me a new car.''

Marty swore under his breath.

"I was out of control by then, of course, although I didn't realize it,'' Donna went on determinedly. She was approaching the worst of what she had to tell. She steeled herself to accept Marty's reaction to it—whatever that reaction might be. "Then, I had my first blackout. And during that blackout... I lost my virginity.''

The blood drained from Marty's face. His body went rigid. "You mean, some guy got you drunk and—''

"No,'' she interrupted fiercely. "*I* got myself drunk and *I* went to bed with a boy I'd barely been introduced to. I was the aggressor, Marty. I was the one who wanted it, or so all my supposed friends told me the day after. And when I heard that, I felt—I felt like a slut.''

"A sl—'' Marty went even paler. His eyes were very, very dark. "Oh, Donna,'' he whispered. He slid his hands up her arms and cupped her shoulders. "That's why you said you weren't easy—that second night we met at Rosa's. That's why you fought against the idea that the two of us damned near went up in flames the first time we kissed. You must have felt— Oh, sweetheart ... sweetheart.''

Marty's use of the endearment stunned Donna. He'd never before, not even at the height of his passion, addressed her by anything other than her name.

Sweetheart.

The clasp of his hands on her shoulders was so warm, so supportive. And the look in his eyes—

It was loving, she realized with a shock. Marty might talk in terms of needing and wanting, but the look she saw in his eyes right now spoke of *loving* and it was directed at her.

For an instant Donna trembled on the brink of telling Marty that she loved him. That she'd probably loved him from the moment their eyes had met at The Funny Farm. But she forced herself back from the brink. She knew she had no right to tell him until she'd finished her story.

"I started acting the way I felt," she resumed. "It was easy to be careless with myself, because I literally couldn't have cared less what happened to me. I was in free-fall. Then I had to confront the possibility that I might be pregnant. The morning I woke up and found out I wasn't, I walked into the bathroom...and I slit my left wrist in three places."

Marty's fingers spasmed. So did his lips. But the expression in his dark brown eyes didn't change. "But you discovered you didn't want to die?" he asked.

Donna felt her mouth twist into a crooked smile, much as Marty's had twisted the night before when he'd told her that his father had only broken his collarbone once.

"No," she answered. "I discovered I couldn't stand the sight of my own blood. I passed out. My head hit the sink before I hit the floor. Donnie—my father found me, unconscious. He was sitting by my bed in the hospital when I finally came to." She moistened her lips. "You said your father cried in front of you once? Well, my father cried in front of me. Then I cried in front of him. And then we both cried together. Afterward, a psychiatrist came in and talked to me. I poured out my whole tale of woe. Then I cried again. And when I finally finished, the psychiatrist told me something I'll remember for the rest of my life. He told me I *wasn't* to blame for the bad things that had happened to me, but I *was* responsible for what I did about them. It was the first time anyone had ever suggested that *I* was responsible for *me*. It was the first time I'd ever thought of myself as being in charge of anything, much less the way I lived my life. It sounds so simple now, but I was like a blind person suddenly being able to see the sun rise. I checked into a rehab clinic the next morning."

She paused, keeping her gaze fixed on Marty's face. "Taking responsibility for what I do—or who I am—has been tough sometimes," she told him honestly. "But I'll take tough times over the alternative any day. I can live with tough times. The alternative would kill me."

There'd been something close to desperation in the way Marty had taken her into his arms after he'd offered her the pieces of his liquor-shattered past the night before. The embrace he enfolded her in now could not have been more different. It was strong and sure and solid. Donna yielded to it with a shuddery sigh of thankfulness and nestled against his hair-whorled chest. The small medallion Sister Mary Pauline had given him pressed gently against her cheek.

She had no idea how long Marty held her, stroking her hair, wordlessly communicating the message that he was there for her as long as she needed or wanted him to be. She clung to him, breathing his scent, savoring his heat, listening to the steady beating of his heart.

The change overtook them very gradually, very naturally. There was no individual instant when the movements of Marty's hands ceased offering comfort and began to caress. There was no single second when Donna's body began to heat and hum with a desire that was as old as Eve. These things just happened and they seemed absolutely right.

The front of his shirt opened, baring her breasts. Donna quivered as she felt Marty's fingers play across her skin. Her nipples puckered, their satiny aureoles turning to nubby velvet.

"Donna, sweetheart . . ." he murmured.

She turned her face up for his kiss.

A split second before his mouth covered hers, Donna offered Marty the final truth about herself.

"I love you," she whispered.

Ten

I love you.

Three words. Three simple, one-syllable words.

Marty Knight told himself he could handle them. God knew, he'd handled a lot worse in his life.

Words couldn't hit.

Words couldn't hurt... much.

I love you.

I can handle it, Marty vowed.

There were a few days—a few perfect, passionate days—when he came very close to believing this might be true.

Then his past returned to haunt him.

"Come on," Donna urged, planting her hands on her hips and tapping her right foot against her tiled kitchen floor. "Tell me. I can handle it."

"I'm sure you can," Marty replied pleasantly, shutting the door of her refrigerator. He crossed to where she was standing and cupped her shoulders with his hands. After a moment, he drew her to him. Dipping his head, he kissed her brow, her nose and her mouth. The first two kisses were light. The third bordered on lusty.

"M-Marty—" Donna stammered when he finally released her.

"I'm sorry," he said, striving for the same pleasant tone he'd used before. Achieving it was almost as difficult as letting go of her had been. "But I can't tell you anything about the outcome of the *Murphy's Law* cliff-hanger. So if you'll excuse me, sweetheart, I'm going to hit the sack."

And with that, he pivoted on his heel and walked out of the kitchen.

Sweetheart, he repeated silently as he padded down the hallway to the elegantly feminine bedroom where he'd spent the previous night.

Five days had passed since he'd spoken that endearment for the first time. He'd spoken it many times since and, in the course of doing so, he'd learned to savor the taste of it on his tongue. He'd also learned to relish the pleasure the word gave Donna. She'd confessed to him just that morning that hearing him call her sweetheart made her go weak in the knees.

Weak in the knees.

Oh, yeah. He could definitely relate to *that* feeling.

Marty reached Donna's bedroom. He stepped inside, shut the door and began shedding his clothes. He had no doubt that Donna would be bursting in on him very shortly. Instinct told him that this was one situation where being caught with his pants down might very well work to his advantage.

The subject of the resolution of the *Murphy's Law* cliff-hanger had first come up about ninety minutes before, while he and Donna were driving home from an enjoyable evening at The Funny Farm. What had begun as teasing chit-chat inspired by an offhand comment from Zeke Peters had escalated into a full-scale battle of wits with no wiles barred by the time they'd gotten back to her house.

Marty shucked his jeans, grinning to himself as he anticipated what was bound to be the satisfying conclusion of this skirmish between the sexes. That this satisfying conclusion would probably be preceded by an explosion didn't faze him a bit. He was certain Donna could be made to see that she'd forced his hand when she'd threatened to use "fiendishly erotic techniques" to obtain the information she was seeking. After all, he'd been on the verge of admitting the truth about what he did, and didn't, know about the *Murphy's Law* cliff-hanger when she'd issued her ultimatum. But once she'd issued it...

Marty cocked an ear, catching the faint sounds that heralded Donna's approach. He hesitated for a split second before deciding to leave his white cotton briefs on. Then he crossed swiftly to Donna's bed and sat down on it.

Bring on the fiendishly erotic techniques, sweetheart, he thought, propping himself up against the headboard and stretching his legs out in front of him. Because I'm going to keep my mouth shut as long as I can.

The bedroom door swung open. Donna stood on the threshold, cheeks flushed, eyes brilliant, breasts straining against the fine fabric of the white silk blouse she was wearing.

"Oh, hello, again," Marty greeted her.

"I know what you're up to, Marty," she declared, stepping into the room and pulling the door shut behind her. She walked gracefully to the side of the bed and looked down at him assessingly. He assumed—well, actually, he *hoped*—she was contemplating her repertoire of fiendishly erotic techniques.

Marty quirked a brow. He rubbed his right hand slowly—he supposed a prurient-minded person might even say suggestively—against his chest. "You know, I seem to recall you saying something similar to me this morning."

"This morning?" Donna pulled down the zipper of the turquoise linen skirt she was wearing. The garment fell to the floor, revealing a champagne silk half-slip. She kicked the skirt aside and started on the small, mother-of-pearl buttons that ran up the front of her blouse.

"Before breakfast. In the shower."

Donna's fingers stilled for an instant. "Oh. That."

"Mmm. To quote you exactly—"

"That won't be necessary!" The interruption was accompanied by a quelling glance. "And what do you mean *before* breakfast? I didn't have time to eat any breakfast this morning, if you'll recall. I was almost late for work, as well."

"At least you were squeaky clean. And, speaking of squeaks—"

"Let's not," Donna cut him off even more decisively than she had a moment before. She finished unbuttoning her blouse and drew it off.

The sheerness of the bra she had on was no surprise. Marty had watched her don it that morning. Nonetheless, his body tightened as he saw her dark rose nipples pout against the lacy fabric of the undergarment. It tightened even more when he recalled that the panties Donna was wearing beneath her half-slip, along with a garter belt and stockings, were equally filmy.

He adjusted his position, his eyes fixed on Donna. She plucked restlessly at the champagne silk that covered her from waist to kneecap. He had the distinct impression that she, too, was thinking about what was underneath her half-slip.

"Yes?" he prompted.

"Yes, what?" Donna's gaze traveled down his body as if drawn by an irresistible force. A soft sound broke from her lips.

"I thought you said we weren't going to talk about squeaks... sweetheart," Marty commented, conscious that his voice was thicker than it had been a few seconds before. He was also conscious that his briefs seemed to be getting briefer. *Much* briefer.

Donna dragged her eyes back up to his face. "I want to know how the *Murphy's Law* cliff-hanger comes out, Marty," she said in a rush. "And I want to know it right now!"

Marty feigned shock. "Is that what this is all about? Now I understand! You came in here intending to loosen my tongue with your fiendishly erotic techniques, didn't you?"

A gasp. "How do you know about my fiendishly—?"

"You threatened me with them when we were driving home from The Funny Farm. Of course, you never specified what any of your techniques were. But if this little striptease is a sample..."

Groaning, Donna sank down on the edge of the bed. She shut her eyes. After a few seconds, Marty edged closer to her. A few seconds after that, he reached for the small fastener that held her bra closed.

"Here," he murmured huskily. "Let me give you a—"

Donna batted his hand away and opened her eyes. "I don't want you to give me anything," she retorted, impaling him with an indignant glare. "Except the inside scoop on the *Murphy's Law* cliff-hanger!"

"I would if I could, but I can't." Marty stroked the hand she'd fended off along the hem of her half-slip, then eased it underneath. Donna bit her lower lip and squirmed, but she didn't protest. Emboldened, he lifted the hand she hadn't batted away up to the front of her bra.

"W-why can't you?" she asked unsteadily.

"I don't know," he answered with a calm he was far from feeling.

The bra fastener opened. So did one of the clasps of her garter belt. Donna sucked in a shuddery breath. "Ex-excuse me?"

Marty repeated himself. He eased the flimsy cups of her bra aside. Two more clasps on her garter belt yielded to his dexterous coaxing.

"You don't know why you can't tell me?" Donna's voice was about a half octave higher than its usual register.

Marty cupped her left breast. "No," he replied, buffing the tip of her nipple with the pad of his thumb. "I know why. I can't tell you because I... don't... know."

The hand that had been exploring beneath Donna's half-slip slowly insinuated itself between her thighs. She arched, gasping, as bold male fingertips began tracing patterns on the sheer fabric of her panties.

"You can't... tell me... because... you don't..." Her expression was as dazed and dreamy as her tone.

Marty knew, to the instant, when Donna registered the implications of the words she was echoing. The dazed and dreamy look disappeared. Her eyes flashed with outrage. But in the midst of the outrage, there was amusement.

"Why you...you—" she choked. It was apparent that at least part of what she was choking on was an urge to laugh. "Are you telling me you can't tell me how the *Murphy's Law* cliff-hanger comes out because you *don't know* how it comes out?"

Marty grinned and nodded, completely unabashed. "The episode hasn't been written—hey!"

Donna conceded to him later that what followed was not especially fiendish. It did, however, involve a number of "techniques" that were highly erotic. These techniques resulted in his ending up flat on his back with her straddling him. They were both breathing heavily by the time this happened.

Marty clasped Donna's body at the waist, then slowly moved his hands upward along her rib cage. He rocked the heels of his palms against the outer curves of her breasts before stroking inward.

"I think this is the point...where you're supposed to say something about...having me in your...power," he advised rather raggedly.

"You're in my power," Donna proclaimed, plainly irked that her big line had been preempted. She rubbed her hands over his chest languidly, mapping every contour. Then she combed her fingers through his chest hair, finding and finessing his taut male nipples. She flicked them lightly with her nails. He groaned. Her lips curved into a wicked little smile. "How does it feel to know that, Marty?"

Marty made no effort to disguise the effect she was having on him. "It feels somewhere between incredibly great and potentially fatal."

"You're not worried?"

"Only that some—ahhh, sweetheart!—vital part is going to give out before you get through killing me."

Donna knelt up and eased backward a bit. She trailed her fingers down Marty's torso and across his belly until she finally reached the elasticized waistband of his briefs. "Any particular vital part?"

Donna sought him. Seduced him. And finally set him free.

With loving care, she clasped the rigid length of his masculine flesh, tracing him from root to tip. Her touch made him tremble like an untried boy.

"Oh, sweetheart."

She adjusted her position once again, balancing herself lightly, holding herself poised like a ballerina. Slowly, ever so slowly, she began to take him into her body. She claimed him inch by inch, sheathing him in burning increments until they were fully mated.

Marty's hands caged Donna's hips with urgent strength, wordlessly commanding her to stay still. She obeyed for a few throbbing seconds, then began to move. He went with her. She was irresistible.

"Marty..."

"Donna..."

In a surging, seamless movement, Marty reversed their positions. He covered Donna's trembling body in a long, hungry caress. The joining he had not believed could be any deeper, any more complete, intensified a hundredfold.

"Yes, sweetheart," he whispered hoarsely. "Oh, yes."

He felt her start to break apart beneath him. His own control vanished less than a second later.

On the morning after they'd first made love, Donna Day had spoken to him about rebirth. Marty Knight's last coherent thought for a long, long time was that this, too, was a form of being reborn—for the better.

Echoes in the darkness.

Voices from the past...

"Don't say that, Marty. Don't ever say that."

"But he is, Mommy. I saw—"

"You don't know what you saw."

"But—"

"Don't ever say that word again. Only bad boys say that word."

"Hey, Marty. Let's go to your house."

"No. My dad is sick."

"Again? He was sick last week!"

"No, sir."

"Betcha I know what he's sick from. I heard my dad say—"

"Shut up. Just shut up!"

"So, Marty. How'd you come to break your collar-bone?"

"I fell off my bike."

"A break like this, you must have been riding pretty fast."

"Yeah. Pretty fast. Really fast."

"Look, son—"

"I fell off my bike, Dr. Peterson. It's my fault!"

"What did the doctor ask you, Marty?"

"Nothing. Leave me alone."

"You know he didn't mean to. You know your father didn't mean—"

"Go away."

"You shouldn't have talked back like you did, Marty. If you hadn't talked back, your father never would have— What did the doctor ask you? What did you tell him?"

"I already said!"

"You can't tell, Marty. We're a family. We love each other. We have to stick together. Your father's sorry. He said he was sorry and he is. So, we'll just forget about this, all right? We'll just wipe it away like it never happened. And it won't happen again. I promise. Do you hear me? I promise. Only you can't tell, Marty. Something bad will happen if you do. You can't ever—"

"—Tell."

Marty awoke with a start. His heart was racing. His muscles were cramped and knotted. His skin was sweat-sheened, yet clammy.

Donna stirred, murmuring in her sleep. She shifted languidly, her body nestling closer to his. She murmured again. Her warm breath misted his nightmare-chilled flesh like a benediction.

Marty felt as if something was cracking open deep inside him. A fissure. A fault line. He couldn't say what it was, but

he knew the break was irreparable. He also knew he was to
blame for it.

Donna murmured a third time. "Mmm," she sighed, then
nuzzled her lips against his chest. "Marty."

"Oh, God . . ." he whispered rawly.

He'd told.

He'd told, and now something bad was going to happen.

Marty shuddered. He tried to control the tremor, but he
couldn't. Nor could he avoid confronting the question it had
shaken loose.

What if the something bad involved Donna?

"Tired?" Marty asked Donna shortly after eight the following Monday evening. They'd finished a casual dinner of
Chinese take-out a short time before. Now they were sitting
side-by-side on one of the chaise longues out on the deck of
his beach house.

"A little," came the soft admission.

Marty put his right arm around Donna. He drew her
close. She leaned her head against his shoulder. The clean
scent of her auburn hair teased his nostrils. Several silken
strands tickled the side of his jaw.

"Long day?" he questioned. She'd made passing reference to a tough counseling session with Sam Collins during
dinner. He knew, from his most recent visit to the Center,
that the youngster was becoming fixated on the idea that he
and his father were going to be reunited when his father was
released from jail roughly three weeks hence.

Donna shifted a little. "A very long day," she affirmed,
then slanted a glance at him. "Preceded by a late night."

Marty stiffened, a pang of guilt slicing through him. His
hunger for her had been almost insatiable the night before.
He'd tried to moderate his need, but he hadn't been able to.
He'd been driven by a sense that each moment with Donna
might be his last. To waste even one of those moments had
been impossible.

"I'm sorry," he said huskily.

Donna blinked, clearly surprised by his apology. "For
what?"

"For keeping you up. I should have let you sleep, sweetheart. I knew you had to go to work."

Her lips parted on a soft ripple of laughter. The sound affected Marty like a caress. It was all he could do not to bend his head and kiss her.

"I wasn't complaining, Marty," she told him.

There was a short silence.

"Of course, I could have done without some of that tossing, turning and talking afterward," Donna added eventually.

Her tone was teasing. Nonetheless, her words made Marty's breath jam at the top of his throat. A moment later he caught the hand that had been caressing him so arousingly.

"I talked?" he asked, his belly knotting.

The question came out sharply. Much more sharply than he'd intended. He saw Donna's smooth brow furrow, watched a hint of wariness enter her lovely green eyes. He berated himself for overreacting.

"Yes," she replied after a fractional pause. "In your sleep."

Marty swallowed. He knew he'd dreamed the night before. He'd dreamed about himself and his father and it had been bad. He'd kept turning into his father and his father had kept turning into him. He'd struggled to stop the transformation, to sever the connection, to cling to his hard-earned sense of who and what he was. But nothing he'd done had helped.

He'd finally clawed his way back to consciousness. His skull had been throbbing sickeningly. The words J.T. Newsom had said to him at Arnold Golding's party had been echoing in his ears like a curse.

Like father, like son.

"Did I say anything—" Marty swallowed a second time, forcing himself to speak lightly "—compromising?"

Donna tilted her head, worry blending with the wariness in her eyes. "Such as?"

He studied her. It's okay, he decided after a few moments. The knot of fear in his gut eased a bit. She doesn't know. Whatever I said, Donna doesn't know.

"Oh, such as the name Trixie," he responded, summoning up a crooked smile. "Or maybe Bubbles or Bambi."

An odd expression flickered across Donna's face. "Now why do those names make me think of that body my head wound up on about a month ago?"

The wry-sounding inquiry threw Marty for a second, then he realized she was referring to the doctored photograph that had marked their debut as a source of tabloid titillation.

"I haven't the faintest idea," he replied. Something about that first photograph nibbled at the edge of his consciousness for an instant, then scurried away before he could pin it down.

There was a pause. Marty waited, braced for the question he knew was coming.

And come, it did.

"What did you really think you might have said, Marty?" Donna asked quietly, disengaging her hand from his. Her gaze was very direct.

Marty didn't want to lie to Donna. But he didn't want to tell her the truth, either. Not yet.

No, he corrected himself. Not *ever*. He'd told her too much already.

"I don't know...exactly," he answered, picking his words carefully. "I didn't even realize I talked in my sleep until you mentioned it." He lifted the hand that had been holding hers until a few seconds before and stroked it gently against the side of her face. She quivered in response to his touch. "I guess I'm still getting used to sharing a bed with someone, sweetheart."

Reminding Donna of the unique place she held in his life was a despicably manipulative thing to do and Marty knew it. But the tactic worked. Donna flushed in response to his last sentence and exhaled on a long, liquid-sounding sigh. She turned her cheek into his palm.

He gathered Donna to him, cradling her body close. His embrace was possessive and protective. He brushed a kiss against her brow. She nestled against him much as she had done the night before.

Yes, indeed. The tactic had worked perfectly. There would be no more questions he couldn't—or wouldn't—answer.

No more, that is, until the next time he spoke in his sleep.

The next time came a little more than forty-eight hours later. It happened shortly before dawn on the day Marty was booked to leave Los Angeles for Las Vegas.

He'd wanted to make the evening before his departure a special one for Donna. They'd dined at an elegantly romantic restaurant, then returned to his beach house and made love.

In the same instant his body convulsed with a pleasure so intense it was almost pain, Marty Knight heard himself cry out the three simple, one-syllable words Donna Day had whispered to him about a week ago.

"I love you."

Echoes in the darkness...

Voices from the past...

Lessons taught too well and learned too thoroughly to be ignored with impunity forever.

"I love you," said Marty's father.

And then he hurt him.

"I love you," said Marty's mother.

And then she allowed him to be hurt.

"I love you," said Marty's lover, the only woman he'd ever hugged to his heart while sleeping.

And then she...

"No," Marty groaned, protesting. "No."

He'd said, "I love you."

Just like his father.

The father who'd hurt him.

Love. Hurt.

First the words.

Then the pain.

He'd said, "I love you."

Just like, just like...

"No," Marty groaned again. He didn't want to hear. He didn't need to hear.

Love. Hurt.

Like father.

"No, please ..."

Like son.

Marty woke. He surged to a sitting position, shuddering violently.

"M-Marty?" Donna's voice was soft and shaky. So were her hands as she reached out and touched him.

"I'm ... all right," Marty lied tautly, clenching his own hands into fists.

He heard the bed sheets rustle as Donna sat up, then felt her slender arms go around him.

"You're trembling," she whispered. She tightened her embrace as though trying to surround him with her fragrant warmth and feminine strength. The sweet weight of her breasts pressed against him.

"I'm all right, sweetheart," he lied for the second time, steeling himself not to take what he so desperately wanted, so desperately needed. "It was only a nightmare."

I love you.

Three words. Three simple, one-syllable words.

Marty Knight had told himself he could handle them.

Now he told himself he'd been wrong.

One week later, Donna Day boarded a plane and went to Las Vegas. The decision to do so was hers and hers alone.

Unfortunately one person found out about her decision before Marty Knight did.

Eleven

"**I** have to go. I've got a plane to catch."

"Just give me one more minute, okay?"

Donna glanced at her watch. Why, oh why, had she picked up the telephone? she asked herself for what seemed like the umpteenth time.

She'd been halfway out her front door when she'd heard the phone start ringing. For a moment she'd been tempted to ignore the shrill summons and allow her answering machine to take a message.

Then her sense of responsibility had asserted itself. Despite the fact that there was a taxi waiting in her driveway with its motor—and meter—running, she hadn't been able to walk away from the possibility that the Center might be trying to contact her.

Dropping her overnight bag and purse, she'd signaled the taxi driver that she'd be out in a minute, then dashed for the phone. She'd braced herself for anything from a high-pressure sales pitch to word that young Sam Collins had buckled under the emotional burdens he was trying to carry.

She'd even braced herself for the possibility that the next voice she'd hear would be Marty's.

It had never occurred to her that the person ringing so insistently would turn out to be her father. She'd realized—too late—that it should have. Heaven knew, she'd been aware that this was the weekend Donnie was scheduled to return to Los Angeles after a series of smashingly successful club dates on the east coast. He'd only mentioned the fact every time he'd phoned her during his absence!

"Donnie, I've given you one more minute about five times already," she pointed out with a trace of asperity.

"Thirty seconds, then," her father bargained. "Put yourself in my shoes. I'm back in L.A. after seven lousy weeks on the road—"

"Lousy?" Donna interrupted, recognizing a variation of what she'd come to think of as the Downtrodden Dad gambit. It was, under the circumstances, preferable to Donnie's Protective Papa routine. "The trade papers said you sold out everywhere you appeared."

A *harrumph* came through the line. Donna could tell Donnie was pleased that she'd kept track of his doings while he'd been away. She could also tell he was annoyed that she'd nailed him on his deliberate misrepresentation of the facts. Her father had little use for accuracy if it undercut the impact of a point he was trying to make.

"Yeah, well. Okay. So maybe not lousy," he conceded. "I'm back in L.A. after seven *long* weeks on the road and all I want to do is see my one and only daughter. I mean, I figured maybe she missed me just a little."

"I missed you," Donna interpolated, poised between exasperation and affection.

"I also figured maybe she wouldn't mind catching me up on her life."

The emotional scales tipped toward exasperation. "Donnie, the only way you could be more caught up on my life is if you were living it."

"You think so?" came the quick retort. "Then how do you explain the fact that I'm still staggering from the bombshell you dropped on me when I asked you why you couldn't have lunch with me today? Some homecoming, Donna Elizabeth. Finding out about you and this comic—"

"Oh, for heaven's sake!" Donna cut in. "The comic's name is Marty Knight and he's been Topic A of just about every telephone conversation you and I have had since that first ridiculous tabloid article came out. So don't give me this bombshell business. You knew I was involved with him."

"Yeah, but I didn't know you were involved enough to go tooting off on a weekend in Vegas! Zeke Peters told me the two of you were—"

"What?"

There was an extremely awkward silence.

"Oh, damn," Donnie finally muttered.

Donna tightened her grip on the telephone. She wasn't really surprised by her father's obviously unplanned revelation. Shocked for an instant, yes. Surprised, no. Donnie had done far worse—or far better, she supposed some might say—in his on-going effort to expiate the guilt she knew he felt about her troubled adolescence. Someday, she hoped, he'd learn to forgive himself for all the terrible things he thought he'd done to her.

"You've been keeping tabs on me through Zeke Peters?" she asked quietly.

"Well . . ."

"Donnie!"

"I know. I know." The words poured out in a rush. "You're thirty years old and you don't need me behaving like some overprotective pain in the butt because I want to make up for all the times I didn't take care of you the way I should have. Well, I'm sorry, Donna. But there's something inside me that says it's better for me to look out for you late than never at all."

Donna sighed. She couldn't argue with such a sentiment. Well, no. Actually she could. And she had. But she'd never come close to altering her father's feelings or alleviating his sense of obligation.

"I've only talked to Zeke three, maybe four times," Donnie went on, plainly determined to confess his transgressions. "The first time was after that damned tabloid piece about the fight at The Funny Farm. Zeke set me straight about what really happened."

"I thought *I'd* done that."

"Yeah, well, he had a different perspective on the situation. Anyway. I decided to stay in touch. Especially after he mentioned that he played Directory Assistance for you and Marty Knight. The last time I phoned him was, oh, maybe two weeks ago. He said the two of you had dropped by The Funny Farm. He told me you looked good together." Donnie's voice softened. "Real good."

Donna felt a sudden pricking of tears at the corners of her eyes. She blinked several times. She knew the night to which her father was referring. Something had happened that night. Something that had altered the tone and texture of her relationship with Marty. She'd gone to bed with a light-hearted lover. She'd woken up with a man who'd seemed weighed down by a burden he couldn't—or wouldn't—share.

Swallowing hard, she checked her watch one more time. She had to go. She had to go *now*.

"Donnie—"

"Yeah, yeah." Her father's tone was brisk, an obvious antidote to the emotionalism of a few moments before. "You've got a plane to catch. Don't let me keep you. Just tell me when you'll be getting back."

Donna hesitated, then opted for honesty. "I'm not sure."

"You're not sure? What does that mean?"

"It means I'm not sure. It depends. I'm taking Monday off from work. But beyond that . . ."

"You and the comic don't have any plans?"

Donna hesitated again. She finally offered an oblique form of the truth. "Not exactly."

Donnie Day was a great many things. Not all of them were good. But his daughter knew that being slow on the uptake had never been one of his failings.

"Geez Louise," he breathed. "He doesn't know you're coming, does he?"

There was a long silence. It was punctuated by the muted blare of a car horn. The taxicab, Donna thought. She opened her mouth to speak. She was forestalled by her father.

"Look," he began intensely. "I realize I don't rate very high on the charts when it comes to giving advice. But this, this going off to Vegas the way you are. It may not be the best thing to do, baby."

Baby.

The word seemed to resonate inside Donna's skull. It had been quite a while since her father had used that endearment when talking to her. The first time he'd employed it had been a little over twelve years ago. She'd been lying in a hospital bed. He'd been sitting beside it, his ruddy cheeks wet with tears.

"I understand that, Daddy," she answered softly. "But I don't have any other choice."

"Donna—"

"Gotta go," she cut in. "I'll call you when I get back."

And then she hung up the telephone and headed off to do what her heart had told her she had to do.

Marty Knight stared at the digital clock sitting on the nightstand next to his bed, calculating how long he had to wait before he could get back on stage.

Ten hours and eighteen minutes.

He closed his eyes and clenched his hands.

He was never going to make it.

He opened his eyes and unclenched his hands.

The read-out on the clock changed.

Ten hours and seventeen minutes.

Marty rolled over onto his back and glared up at the gilt-trimmed ceiling of his lavishly appointed hotel suite.

He was falling apart. He couldn't sleep. He couldn't eat. The only time he felt he had any semblance of control over his life was when he was performing. And even then he was so far out on the edge . . .

He'd been brought to his present condition by the knowledge that he had to end his relationship with Donna Day. He had no choice. He'd *never* had a choice. He had to end it.

The only question was how.

He wanted it to be quick.

He wanted it to be clean.

He wanted there to be no opportunity for questions.

Oh, hell. What he *really* wanted was for Donna to break off with him!

He knew she'd realized that something had gone wrong between them. He'd seen it in her eyes before he'd left for Las Vegas. He'd heard it in her voice every time they'd spoken during the past eight days. The problem was, she plainly believed that what had gone wrong was fixable.

But it wasn't.

Marty sat up. He thrust his fingers back through his hair, conscious that his hands weren't entirely steady. Then again, neither was his pulse.

This was the part he'd been worried about from the very start of his involvement with Donna. And he'd been right to be worried. If only he hadn't—

The telephone that was sitting next to the clock shrilled suddenly. Marty started violently at the sound. The phone rang a second time. He leaned over and picked up the receiver with a hand that was even shakier than it had been a few seconds before.

"Hello?"

"Marty Knight?"

The voice was male. It was also vaguely familiar.

"Yeah," he affirmed after a pause.

"This is Donnie Day."

Marty's breath jammed at the top of his throat. His heart lurched sickeningly. He found himself reaching for the medallion he'd gotten from Sister Mary Pauline so many years before.

"Is it Donna?" he demanded harshly. "Has something happened to Donna?"

"No. She's okay," the man on the other end of the line replied. His tone was odd, as if he'd been taken aback by the intensity of Marty's inquiry. "At least, I *think* she's okay."

"You think?" Marty echoed sharply, his entire body tensing. How the hell could a father say he thought his daughter was okay? Didn't he *know?* "What does that mean?"

"It means—" the sound of a throat being cleared came through the line "—Donna's headed for Vegas."

For a moment Marty's brain simply refused to process this last sentence. It shut down. Went into shock, or out on strike.

"Donna's coming here?" he finally managed to echo.

"Yeah."

Donna. Coming to Vegas.

Donna.

"She'll kill me if she ever finds out I called you," Donnie Day went on heavily. "But I, well, let's just say I understand how things can get when you're on the road, okay? I'm not making any judgments. God knows, I don't have a right to judge anybody. Even so—"

"You don't want Donna walking in on something," Marty summed up brutally. His heart was thudding like a bass drum. His temples were throbbing. The odd thing was, he felt no sense of offense at the assumptions Donnie Day had apparently made about the kind of man he was.

"Exactly."

Marty Knight suddenly knew how to do what he had to do. He had no choice.

"What time is she supposed to get here?" he asked.

"This going off to Vegas the way you are. It may not be the best thing to do, baby."

Donna sighed and closed the magazine she'd been pretending to read for the past ninety minutes. She turned her head and stared blindly out the small window to her left.

"I understand that, Daddy. But I don't have any other choice."

She sighed again. The decision to go to Las Vegas, unannounced, had not been an easy one for her to make. She'd wrestled with it for nearly a week after Marty's departure before she'd reached the conclusion that she had to do it. Her only other options were untenable.

She was going to Las Vegas because she had to try to heal the breach she knew had opened between her and the man she loved. And if she couldn't heal it, then she was at least going to try to make some sense of it.

What she and Marty had had together had been good. No. More than good. It had been just about perfect. The happiness she'd experienced during the first few days after they'd consummated their relationship had been beyond her ability to put into words.

And Marty had shared in her indescribable happiness. Although she had a great many doubts about a great many things, Donna had no doubts about that. Their emotional union had been as ecstatically complete as their physical one.

But then something had changed. Less than a week after they'd become intimate, she'd begun detecting signs of stress in Marty. They'd been subtle at first, but they'd grown increasingly obvious with each passing day...and night. It had become clear to her that Marty was locked in a struggle with himself.

She'd sought to understand the why of what was happening, but to no avail. She'd tried to soothe, but with no success. Although there'd been no overt rejection, she'd met resistance at every turn. She'd discovered that the defenses she'd believed had come tumbling down for good had been rebuilt.

Not just rebuilt, but made stronger than ever.

She'd let herself hope that the three-word confession Marty had cried out the night before he'd left for Las Vegas would ease the conflict she sensed roiling inside him. She knew, from personal experience, that peace could stem from saying "I love you."

It's going to be all right, she'd told herself as she'd drifted off to sleep, secure in the circle of her lover's strong arms. *Finally...finally, it's going to be all right.*

But it hadn't been all right. Shortly before dawn, she'd been awakened by the sound of Marty groaning like a man suffering the tortures of the damned. In the space of a few hammering heartbeats, her faith in the future had been shattered.

What had followed *had* been rejection. While Marty hadn't turned away from her touch, he'd evaded her questions and avoided her eyes. He'd steadfastly refused to tell her what was troubling him. Shaken by his withdrawal, she'd pursued the matter up to the moment of his departure. She'd broached it during the calls he made to her from

Las Vegas, as well. But no matter how many times she tried—

"Excuse me, ma'am."

Donna dropped out of her reverie. Her head snapped left. "Yes?" she said to the flight attendant who'd addressed her.

"We've begun our descent into Las Vegas," the young woman stated. "You need to bring your seat to its upright position."

Donna fumbled with the button on the armrest. Her fingers were trembling. "How long?"

The flight attendant smiled. "Not very. We'll be arriving right on schedule."

Marty raked a hand through his hair and surveyed the voluptuous blonde who'd just glided out of his hotel bathroom wearing nothing but a black satin teddy and a frown. Her name was Patricia Elizabeth Wrzesniewski. He'd met her at St. Cecilia's in Chicago nearly seventeen years ago. Like him, she'd been something of a misfit. But her failure to fit in had been a lot more obvious than his. Patricia Elizabeth Wrzesniewski had been referred to as "Fatsy Patsy" back then.

She wasn't referred to that way these days. Roughly sixty pounds lighter and fifteen shades blonder than she'd been back in Chicago, Fatsy Patsy Wrzesniewski was now known as Trish Wren. She was one of the most sought-after show girls in Vegas.

They'd picked up the thread of their acquaintanceship six years ago, when Marty had been booked into one of the lounges at the casino-hotel where Trish worked. Flying in the face of a lot of odds, they'd developed a casual, buddy-buddy kind of relationship. There had never ever been anything sexual between them.

"I've thought about it some more," Trish announced, fluffing her cornsilk-colored hair with her immaculately manicured right hand. "And I'm sorry, Marty. But this practical joke of yours just is *not* going to be funny."

"Trust me, Trish," Marty responded tersely.

"Trust me, he says," Trish echoed. "That rates right up there with 'Give me your number, I'll call you' on the credibility charts, Marty. Now I *know* there's something weird about this setup." She crossed to his unmade, king-size bed with the confident grace of a woman accustomed to strutting her stuff in public and sat down.

Marty began prowling around the room. He darted a glance at the digital clock on the nightstand.

Seven hours and nine minutes until he got back on stage, he told himself, sucking in a deep breath. But before he did, he was going to have to give the performance of his life in front of an audience of—

He realized Trish was speaking to him again. "What?"

The blonde gave him an assessing look. "I asked you what this friend of yours is like," she said. "You know. The one you claim is going to bust a gut when he catches us in flagrante delicto?"

Marty fought to discipline his features. "Just a friend," he answered. He wondered how many more lies he'd have to tell before his tongue became inured to the rancid taste of deception.

"Cute?"

"Not your type."

"Mmm."

There was a pause. Marty kept prowling.

"I'm not peeling down any further than this," Trish declared after nearly a minute of silence.

Marty checked himself in mid-stride. "Huh?"

"I know I said I'd help you with this stupid gag and I will. But I'm *not* taking anything else off."

"Fine."

"And I want you to keep your pants on."

The pants in question were jeans. They were also Marty's sole item of attire at the möment. He shrugged his acquiescence and started moving around the room again. He didn't need to strip down to his skivvies to get this job done. With the help of a strategically positioned bedsheet, having his upper body bare would be sufficient.

"I wonder what Donna Day would say if she walked in right now," Trish mused aloud.

There was no way Marty could control his initial reaction to the sound of Donna's name. He stopped dead in his

tracks, his heart hammering. Fortunately, his back was to
the bed, preventing Trish from seeing the look he knew must
be on his face.

"Marty?"

He did what he could to arrange his features into something approaching a neutral expression. Then he forced
himself to turn around. He was going to have to be very
careful. While a lot of men figured Trish Wren for a bimbo,
he knew she was as shrewd as she was shapely. Being blond
and bosomy didn't mean she was a brainless woman any
more than being padded in fat had meant she'd cushioned
against emotional bruises when she'd been an adolescent.

"What do you know about Donna Day?" he asked, trying for an even tone. He felt as though he was strangling.

"Only what I read in the papers while I'm waiting in the
checkout line at the supermarket," Trish answered. The skin
between her perfectly plucked eyebrows pleated. "Oh, look.
It was just a wisecrack, Marty. The comment about what
Donna Day would think, I mean. I, well, what can I say? I
feel kind of connected to her, you know?"

No, Marty didn't know. And he wasn't at all certain he
wanted to.

"Because of the picture," Trish elaborated.

"The picture?"

Trish rolled her smoky violet eyes. "In the paper, about
a month and a half ago. My body? Her head?"

Comprehension didn't dawn; it detonated. And it rocked
Marty right down to his heels in doing so. "That was *you* in
that phonied-up photograph?"

"From the neck down, yeah." Trish cocked her head.
"You didn't think it was her did you?"

"No. Of course not." Marty forked his fingers through
his mussed-up hair. He fired a glance at the telephone.
Where the hell was Donna? he wondered. What if something had happened?

"You didn't know," Trish said in a voice that held equal
parts of astonishment and accusation.

"What?"

"You had no idea that was my body! Marty, I like the fact that you relate to me as a human being and not a pair of boobs, but there *are* limits."

Marty's mind suddenly flashed back to the uneasy conversation he and Donna had had out on the deck of his beach house the Monday before his departure for Las Vegas. He'd made a lame joke about mentioning names like Trixie, Bubbles or Bambi in his sleep. She'd responded with a brief reference to the doctored photo. He, in turn, had experienced a fleeting sense that there was something familiar about the picture, but he'd never figured out what it was.

"But you and I've never—" he started, remembering the apparently intimate embrace the photograph had depicted.

"Of course, we've *never,*" Trish cut in with a trace of asperity. "But the last time you came to Vegas, you took me to a party because my date for the evening—a creep, as most of my dates seem to be—had stood me up. Remember? The big birthday bash? And on the way in—"

"The heel of your shoe broke and I caught you when you toppled over," Marty finished as the episode surfaced from the depths of his memory.

"Uh-huh. The place was crawling with paparazzi. There was a picture of the two of us making like Siamese twins in one of the tabloids about a week later. A girl from the Follies showed it to me. It was the same picture they stuck Donna Day's head on." She grimaced. "What's that saying? Something about never being able to escape the past? I mean—"

At that point the telephone on the nightstand rang. Marty crossed to it in three swift strides. He picked the receiver up, put it to his ear, listened for ten seconds, then dropped it back in the cradle.

"Marty?"

"It's show time, Trish. Get into the bed."

Something's wrong, Donna thought as she walked away from the registration desk at the hotel where Marty was staying. Even more wrong than she'd feared.

Her fingers tightened on the strap of her overnight bag.

Then again, maybe something was right. More right than she'd dared to dream might be possible after the past two and a half weeks.

"Mr. Knight asked us to send you straight up, Miss Day," the registration clerk had declared less than a minute before, mercifully interrupting her awkward attempt to explain who she was and why she needed to know what room Marty Knight was staying in.

"He told— Marty's expecting m-me?" she'd stammered, unable to believe she'd heard the dapperly dressed young man correctly.

"I guess so. Would you like a bellman to carry your bag up to your room?"

She'd had to struggle to come up with an appropriate answer to this inquiry. "Uh, no. No, thank you. I can manage myself."

The clerk had produced a pleasant smile and a room key. "It's Suite 1825. The elevators are to the right. Enjoy your stay."

Donna shook her head, trying to make sense of the exchange at the front desk. There was no way Marty could have known she was coming to Las Vegas—was there? After all, she hadn't made the decision to do so until after the last time she'd spoken with him.

At least, not consciously.

Had he sensed what had been in her heart and mind during that final conversation? she wondered. Had he anticipated the action she'd feel compelled to take?

Had he *hoped?*

Donna reached the bank of elevators. One car was open and waiting. She got on and pressed the button marked 18. The doors whispered shut.

After a moment, the elevator began to rise.

Mr. Knight asked us to send you straight up, Miss Day.

The question was, straight up to what?

Afterward, Marty told himself that he'd gotten most of what he'd wanted.

What happened in Suite 1825 was quick. And clean. And even though it involved some questions, they didn't come from Donna.

"Do you want me to move around and make noise?" Trish asked uncomfortably.

"Just do—" Marty yanked the sheet up to his waist "—what comes naturally."

"Well, what comes naturally is my getting out of this bed and—"

There was a knock at the door to his suite.

"Shh."

Quick and clean.

A second knock.

The sound of the door to his suite being opened.

"Marty?"

Donna's voice. It was soft and sweet and it sliced through Marty like a surgeon's blade.

Love. Hurt.

First the words.

Then the pain.

"Wha—?" Trish gasped and started struggling to sit up. Marty stilled her. Silenced her.

"Marty? Are you here?"

God, he thought savagely. Just get this over with!

Positioned as he was, Marty couldn't see the door that connected the suite's entertainment area with its bedroom. But he did hear the door open.

He shifted his body. He made a few sounds. He felt Trish dig her nails into his shoulders.

"Marty? It's Don—"

A shuddery intake of breath followed by an unbearable moment of silence. Then, an anguished whisper, "I'm sorry."

The bedroom door closed.

A few seconds later he heard the suite's outer door being opened . . . then shut.

Marty Knight felt his soul dying by inches.

It was slow.

And it was dirty.

And he knew he deserved it.

* * *

Scant minutes later.

Marty was standing at the well-stocked wet bar in the suite's entertainment area. He'd told Trish to get into her clothes and go. She'd told him there was nothing she'd rather do.

"You bastard."

He reached for a bottle of whiskey and a glass. He didn't turn around.

"You set her up and you used me to do it. You *bastard*."

He cracked the seal on the liquor bottle, then carefully unscrewed the top. Still, he didn't turn around.

"I thought I knew you, Marty. I thought— How could you do something like this?"

He'd had no choice.

"Leave it alone, Trish," he said flatly. He poured one, two, three inches of booze into the glass he'd selected.

He wrapped his fingers around the glass. He lifted the glass to his lips.

The smell of whiskey.

The stench . . . of whiskey.

Funny. It didn't seem to bother him.

"No, I won't leave it alone!" Trish exploded. "Dammit, Marty, I want to know why you—"

Marty pivoted around so quickly that some of the Scotch slopped out of the glass and onto his hand. His only gauge of what he must look like was the appalled expression that appeared on Trish's face.

"What's the matter?" he asked. His voice sounded strange to him. "Haven't you ever seen a guy take a drink before?"

Trish's cheeks were pale. Her eyes were huge. "Yeah," she whispered. "But the guy was never you."

"Well, it's me now." Marty laughed a little. He saw Trish flinch at the sound that issued from his throat.

"Marty, for God's sake—" she began.

"Like father like son," he cut in, raising his glass in a mocking salute.

"W-what?"

He turned away from her and back to the wet bar.

Quick. Clean. And no opportunity for questions.

"Get out, Patsy," he said harshly.

"But—"

He felt her touch his shoulder. He stiffened at the contact. *"Get the hell out."*

After a few moments, she did.

Except for one incident, Donna's memory of what happened between the time she found the man she loved in bed with another woman and the time she arrived back in Los Angeles was never very clear.

That one incident involved a glass of champagne.

Her only goal when she'd left Suite 1825 had been to go home. She'd taken a taxi to the Las Vegas airport where she'd discovered that there was an L.A.-bound flight departing in less than twenty minutes.

There'd been just one seat available. It had been in First Class. She'd booked it and dashed for the gate.

She'd gone to the lavatory, where she'd been violently ill, as soon as the plane's seatbelt sign had been turned off. The glass of champagne had been waiting when she'd finally returned to her seat.

"Wh-what's this?" she questioned, pointing to the champagne.

"You looked a little distraught, dearie," the silver-haired woman occupying the seat next to hers explained. "I thought a bit of the bubbly might settle you down. Besides—" she shrugged a plump shoulder clad in a particularly vivid shade of turquoise polyester "—it comes with the ticket."

Donna opened her mouth to say she didn't drink. The admission died in her throat. She murmured her thanks, then slid into her seat.

It had been a long time—a *lifetime*, it seemed—since Donna Elizabeth Day had been tempted to take a drink. But looking at the glass of champagne...

Take a sip, the champagne urged. *Just one tiny sip.*

She swallowed. There was a vile taste in her mouth.

You know it will help, the champagne lured.

She clenched and unclenched her hands.

Poor Donna, the champagne sympathized. *You don't have to hurt like this, you know.*

Donna closed her eyes.

Marty, she thought. Oh, God. Marty.

He'd wanted her sent . . . straight up.

She loved him! She loved him so much! What had she done to deserve this kind of betrayal?

Marty . . . in bed with another woman.

Moving. Making sounds deep in his throat.

His hair, dark. Hers, sunshine light.

Donna bit her lower lip.

The sight of his naked back. The supple skin. The sleek male muscles rippling beneath.

Donna's palms and fingertips tingled with the memory of how it felt to stroke Marty's naked back. The back she'd seen another woman caressing . . .

Oh, God!

Donna opened her eyes.

Never mind about him, the champagne counseled. *I'll take care of you. You know I can. Depend on me.*

Donna touched the base of the glass.

That's it. Come on. Just a sip to start.

She ran a finger up and down the stem of the glass. Her breath was sawing in and out. She licked her lips.

Bubbles danced on the surface of the sparkling beverage, bursting like teeny tiny balloons. She could recall the sensation of such bubbles bursting on her tongue.

You don't have to feel this way, Donna, the champagne reminded her. *You don't have to feel at all.*

Donna traced the rim of the glass.

Around.

And around.

And around again.

Wouldn't it be nice to be numb? the champagne asked.

Numb.

Numb.

Wouldn't it be nice to be numb?

"No," Donna whispered suddenly.

"Dearie?" the woman sitting next to her queried.

What do you mean—no? the champagne challenged.

"I mean *no*," Donna stated, withdrawing her hand.

"Dearie, is something wrong?"

Donna looked at her seat mate. "Yes," she said starkly. She sucked in a deep breath, trying to control the trembling that threatened to overtake her. "But this—" she nodded at the suddenly silent glass of alcohol "—isn't going to make it any better."

Marty never knew how many times he brought the glass of whiskey he'd poured to his mouth after Trish left. Maybe ten times. Maybe twenty. Maybe more.

The last time he actually closed his lips over the rim.

Drink it, he told himself.

Love. Hurt.

First the words.

Then the pain.

Drink it.

Like father, like son.

Like father ... like—

"*No!*" The word seemed to erupt from the very core of his being. He slammed the glass down so hard it shattered. He realized he was shaking all over. "Dammit, *no!* It doesn't, it doesn't have to be ... like that. It doesn't ... have ... to ..." The shaking got worse. "Oh, G-God ..." He was gasping like a drowning man. "Oh, God ... oh *Donna.*"

He'd driven the woman he loved away.

He'd betrayed his future because he was afraid of his past.

In that moment, Marty Knight knew what it felt like to hit bottom.

A moment later, he knew what it felt like to weep for the first time since he'd been seven years old.

Twelve

Somehow, Donna made it through the remainder of the weekend. She was back behind her desk at the Better Day Center for Children early Monday morning. That's where Lydia Foster found her.

"I didn't think you were going to be in today," Lydia said.

Donna kept her eyes on the paperwork she was sorting through. "Change of plans," she replied tersely. While she hadn't told Lydia why she'd wanted this particular day off, she suspected her friend had made an accurate guess about the reason.

"Do you want to talk about it?"

"No."

There was a pause. Donna continued shuffling forms. She felt her throat tighten and the bridge of her nose start to clog with unshed tears.

She wasn't going to cry. She *wasn't*. She'd done enough of that over the weekend.

"Donna..."

Lydia's tone was very odd. Unable to prevent herself, Donna looked up at the other woman. Lydia's attractive face was a study in conflict.

Donna swallowed hard. "What is it?" she asked, grateful that her voice was steady.

No answer.

"Lydia?"

Lydia opened her mouth as if to say something, then shut it again.

She knows, Donna thought. Somehow, she knows.

"Lydia?" she questioned again.

The other woman shook her dark head, her distinctive features coalescing into an expressionless mask. "Nothing," she responded. "I just..." She shook her head again. "If you need to talk, I'm here, all right?"

Donna nodded once, knowing that what she needed and what she was going to do were two entirely different things.

The next evening, she met her father at one of Hollywood's hottest restaurants.

"Are you *sure* you don't want to talk about it?" Donnie Day asked.

Donna dragged a tortilla chip back and forth across a bowl of what their waiter had touted as "the best" guacamole in Los Angeles County. Compared with the zesty avocado and tomato she and Marty had shared at La Cocina de Rosa, the stuff was as flavorless as library paste.

Then again, "flavorless" pretty much summed up most of what little she'd eaten during the past seventy-two hours.

"Yes," she said quietly, keeping her gaze fixed on the bowl of guacamole. "I'm sure."

She would have avoided this dinner if there'd been any way to do so, but there hadn't been. Although she'd been able to screen her father's calls at home, she hadn't been able to do so at the Center. He'd finally learned of her return to Los Angeles that morning when he'd phoned there. They'd had a brief conversation in which Donnie had made it abundantly clear that he was not going to allow himself to be put off, put on or put down.

"At least tell me what happened in Vegas."

"No, Donnie."

There was a pause.

"Dammit, I feel like it's my fault!"

Donna's head came up. She stared at the salt-and-pepper-haired man sitting opposite her in disbelief. "*Your* fault?" she echoed. "How in heaven's name could it be—"

She broke off abruptly, her pulse stuttering. There was something about her father's expression that told her his last statement had been more than a manifestation of his free-floating sense of guilt about her.

"Donna—" he began, shifting in his seat.

Donna leaned forward. "Why would it be your fault?"

"I—" Donnie's throat worked for a second or two "—called him."

Donna caught her breath. There was no need for Donnie to identify who the "him" was.

"When?"

"Last Saturday," came the awkward admission. "After I talked to you. I was worried. I mean, okay! Okay! I shouldn't have. But I was worried about you."

Donna swallowed hard. If she'd been asked to identify the emotions she was experiencing at this moment, she would have been unable to. There were too many of them and they were too contradictory and confusing to sort out. "You...didn't want me walking in on something."

Donnie's gray eyes narrowed. His mouth thinned for a moment. "That's what he said."

Donna's throat seemed to close up. Her stomach clenched like a fist. Her heart began banging against the inside of her chest as though it was trying to break through her ribs.

Mr. Knight asked us to send you straight up, Miss Day.
Marty...in bed with another woman.
Mr. Knight asked us to send you straight up, Miss Day.
Moving. Making sounds deep in his throat.
His hair, dark. Her hair, sunshine light.
Mr. Knight asked us to send you straight up, Miss Day.
Marty...in bed with—

"Donna?" Donnie reached across the table and took her left hand in his right.

Then it all became clear to her. "It was a set-up," she whispered, barely registering the comforting squeeze of her father's fingers. "It was all a setup."

"What was a setup?"

Marty... in bed with another woman.

He'd known she'd been coming.

He'd wanted her to walk in on something. He'd wanted her to walk in on something that would make her turn around and walk—no, *run!*—away.

I love you! he'd cried out at the peak of his passion the night before he'd left her to go to Las Vegas.

He'd meant it. With every cell in her brain and body, with every fiber of her soul, she *knew* that he'd meant it. Yet only hours later, before dawn the next morning...

Marty had said no in his sleep. She'd heard him. Over and over he'd said no. He'd said it in protest. In denial. In anguish.

A nightmare, he'd claimed when she'd asked him. Only a nightmare.

Mr. Knight asked us to send you straight up, Miss Day.

Marty... in bed with another woman.

Why?

Why had he done such a thing?

"Baby?" her father questioned, tightening his grip on her hand.

Donna shook her head, her auburn hair shifting back and forth against her nape. "I don't want to talk about it, Daddy."

The following afternoon, Donna sat in her office at the Better Day Center for Children.

"Sam—"

Belligerent brown eyes bored into concerned green ones. "No!"

"Sam, we have to talk about this."

"No!" The boy made an angry gesture of denial. His short-cropped hair bristled. "You don't understand. *Nobody* at this stupid place understands!"

Donna took a steadying breath. "I understand you think you should be with your father after he's released from jail next week."

"That's the way it's s'posed to be!"

Time to push, Donna decided. "Is that what you *want*?" she asked.

Sam stiffened. His features turned pinched and pasty as he lost most of the color in his face. For a second, he was unable to hide what Donna had always known he was: a terribly frightened child who would do just about anything to keep the world from learning how truly vulnerable he was.

Then, with heartbreaking swiftness, he slammed his defenses up.

"That's the way it's *s'posed* to be!" he repeated fiercely. He clenched his stubby-fingered hands into fists and glared at her. "Me and him...we're *s'posed* to be together!"

"But is that what you want, Sam? Is that what you really want?"

The question rocked him. For a split second, it seemed he might break down. Then, defiantly, *"He's my dad!"*

"Sam—"

"I don't want to talk about it!"

The statuesque blonde who stood in the doorway of Donna's tiny office roughly forty-eight hours later *did* want to talk. She had come hundreds of miles to do so.

"Donna, there's a Trish Wren here to speak with you," the Center's receptionist had informed her a minute or two before.

"Trish Wren?" she'd repeated blankly. The name had meant nothing to her.

"Yes. Trish Wren from Las Vegas. She says it's very important. She says it's about Marty Knight."

Donna had bitten the inside of her lower lip so hard at that point that she'd drawn blood. "I'll see her," she'd responded after a moment. "Will you send her down to my office, please?"

"Miss Wren?" Donna questioned, slowly getting to her feet. She was dimly surprised that her knees could support her weight. She knew exactly who this strikingly sexy woman was. What she didn't know—and wasn't at all certain she wanted to find out—was why this woman had come to see her.

"Right," the blonde said, affirming her identity with a nod. "Trish Wren." She studied Donna for several moments, the expression in her smoky violet eyes disconcertingly direct. Finally, she said, "You know who I am, don't you?"

"I—" Donna cleared her throat "—I think I recognize your hair."

Trish grimaced and fluffed her fair tresses self-consciously. "Yeah. I'll bet you probably do."

Donna remained silent for a few seconds. She found herself surveying the other woman very carefully. Strangely, she felt no hostility toward her. Rather, she was experiencing a curious sense of, well, not *kinship* exactly, but close to it. There was something . . . special . . . about Trish Wren. In an odd way, she reminded Donna of Lydia Foster.

Suddenly a piece of a conversation she'd had weeks before came back to her.

That picture is the most blatant composite shot I've ever seen in my life, she'd told Lydia Foster through gritted teeth. *It's so phony it's almost funny! Why anyone could have the unmitigated gall to stick* my *head on some* other *woman's body—*

Hey, at least it's an attractive body.

Her breath came out in a rush. She met Trish Wren's questioning gaze. "I think . . . I think I may recognize more than your hair."

Trish's full lips twisted a bit. "'Knight In Fight For Day's Daughter,'" she quoted. "Yeah. That was me. You've got a better eye than Marty, Miss Day."

Donna flinched at the sound of Marty's name. She couldn't help it.

The other woman took a step forward, distress vivid on her features. "It's not what you think!" she said urgently. "The picture—please. *Please!* And what you walked in on— God, I know what it looked like. But it wasn't. I swear to you, it wasn't what you think!"

"How do you know what I think?"

Trish didn't bother to answer this. She didn't need to. The look on her face clearly communicated the conviction that *any* woman would know the content of Donna's thoughts.

"Did—" Donna swallowed convulsively "—did M-Marty ask you to come here?"

"No." The denial was instant and unequivocal.

"Then why—?"

"Well, for one thing, I don't want you to think I'm a slut."

Donna shuddered slightly at the last word. "I don't think that, Miss Wren," she said after a moment. She realized she was telling the truth.

Trish's expression became very intent. She took another step forward. "Then you don't think Marty and I—?"

Donna licked her lips. "I did," she admitted. "But I don't now." In point of fact, she'd stopped thinking Marty had been unfaithful to her two nights before when she'd learned that he'd been forewarned about her arrival.

There was a short, sharp pause.

"Can I sit down?" Trish finally asked.

Donna gestured to the chair in front of her desk. "Please."

"Thanks."

There was another pause as Trish got settled. Donna reseated herself very carefully and waited.

"I—I went back and forth and back and forth about coming to see you," Trish finally confessed. "But I finally decided I had to."

"How did you know where to find me?"

"Oh, that was easy. I've been reading about you in the tabloids. Not that I believe much of what gets printed but, well, one of the articles talked about you working here. At this place for kids with problems. That helped me make up my mind about coming. I mean, Marty's got problems, Miss Day."

"He's told you about them?"

Trish looked startled. "No," she answered. "God, no. It's—okay. Look. Marty and I go way back. We went to school together."

"You went to St. Cecilia's?" Donna tried, fleetingly, to imagine Trish Wren in a parochial school uniform.

The other woman seemed to divine the direction of her thoughts. "I've changed a lot since I was a kid, Miss Day. I was Patricia Elizabeth Wrzesniewski back then. Popularly—or maybe I should say unpopularly—known as Fatsy Patsy."

"Oh."

"Marty was the class clown. Fast. Funny. And sharp. Man, was he sharp! We had some pretty tough guys in school but they all learned to steer clear of him. I mean, a couple of them tried to beat on him once or twice. They thought he was some kind of chicken because he just let them pound away. He never fought back. But then, afterward, he zinged them with a few comments. It was, well, he really nailed them. And the comments got around, you know? They stuck like glue. And pretty soon, everybody in the school was laughing at those bullying jerks. Anyway. It would have been really easy for Marty to pick on me. Just about everybody else did. I was a *big* target in more ways than one. But in all the time we were in school together, he never made a single joke about me. I got the feeling he understood how much misery I was carrying around. Well, he never *said* anything, you understand. And, Lord knows, I never brought it up. But I think the reason he was nice to me was because he was carrying a lot of misery around, too. I mean, there was talk around school about his father being a drunk. And, well, I, uh, had the feeling his home was pretty much of a battle zone when his old man was boozing."

Donna said nothing. It was obvious that Trish Wren had been endowed with a lot more than a voluptuous figure.

Trish cocked her head to one side, her gaze shrewd and steady. "You know, don't you." It wasn't a question. "You know all about it. He told you. Marty *told* you."

"I know some," Donna corrected after a moment. "But I don't know why he did what he did . . . with you. Not for sure."

Trish's expression turned grim. "He told me it was a practical joke."

"What?"

"He called me up and said he needed my help with a gag he wanted to play on some friend of his who was coming in from L.A. I was half-zonked. I mean, he'd woken me up out of a sound sleep. And, like an idiot, I told him I'd help. I started having second thoughts as soon as I hung up the phone. I was on about fifth or sixth thoughts by the time I got to his room. And then he said, 'Trust me.' Now, normally, when a guy says 'Trust me' I start heading for the exit, you know. But this was Marty and, well..."

"You trusted him."

"Yeah. But when I realized—" Trish shook her head, plainly trying to shunt the memory out of her mind. "I was so...God!...I was so *angry* afterward. I called him a bastard and a whole bunch of other things. But then he turned around and I got a good look at his face and..." Trish broke off, shuddering.

Donna went cold. "What do you mean?"

"Well, he was at the wet bar in the other room in the suite—"

"Marty was *drinking?*" Her voice came close to shredding on the last word.

"He was going to. Things got...I don't know. Very *weird*. Almost scary. I mean, I wasn't scared of Marty. But, well, he lifted up the glass he had. Like he was making a toast, you know? And then he said in this really strange voice, 'Like father, like son.'"

Like father, like son.

Donna's heart skipped a beat. She'd heard those words before. She knew where and she knew when.

Deep down you're scared you're just like him, aren't you, Marty? J.T. Newsom had taunted him. *A loser. An abuser. A ready-made boozer...*

No. Marty couldn't believe those words. Not anymore!

He *couldn't*.

Could he?

"What happened then?" she asked.

"He told me to get the hell out and I did."

"You just left him there to get drunk?"

Trish stiffened as though she'd been slapped across the face. "Look—"

"No. No. I'm sorry, Miss Wren," Donna apologized quickly, appalled that she'd lashed out at the other woman. "I'm sure he didn't give you any other choice."

Trish remained silent for several seconds. "I would have stayed if I'd thought I could have helped," she admitted slowly. "But I knew I couldn't."

Donna nodded. "I understand."

"I'm pretty sure he didn't get drunk."

"You are?"

"Yeah. I checked with a friend of mine. Suzanne. She's in the line at the hotel where Marty's playing. Anyway, she told me he seemed totally straight when he went on Saturday night. And Suzanne's got a real instinct about that sort of thing. She also told me Marty was terrific during both shows. It's been the same every night since."

Donna slumped in her seat.

Trish leaned forward.

"Look, Donna," she began, then hesitated. "Is it all right if I call you Donna?"

"Yes. Of course."

"Okay. And you call me Trish. Or Patsy. Or whatever you want. Anyway, look. I know what Marty did hurt you. I mean, if it'd been me in the doorway and you in the bed, well…" The blonde grimaced eloquently. "Frankly, there's a part of me that feels like I'm betraying the sisterhood— you know, women looking out for women so we don't *all* get screwed at the same time?—by saying what I'm about to say. But, I think you should know that however much Marty hurt you, he hurt himself more. Much more. Like I said, the look on his face when he turned around was, well, if I never see another look like it again as long as I live, it'll be too soon. It wasn't the look of a guy who'd just gotten done dumping some girl he didn't give a damn about. I've seen that kind of look on guys' faces before, believe me! It was, well, okay. Bottom line. In some twisted way, I think Marty did what he did because he loves you."

Donna dropped her gaze. She inhaled shakily. "So—so do I," she whispered, blinking against the needling pressure of unshed tears.

"And you love him, don't you?"

Donna nodded, not trusting her voice.

"Then, will you come back to Vegas with me?"

Donna looked up, flushing. "Is *that* why you came here?"

"Yeah," Trish said simply. "Will you?"

She wanted to say yes. More than anything else in the world, Donna Elizabeth Day wanted to say yes. But listening to Trish had brought all her inchoate suspicions about what had driven Marty to do what he'd done into focus.

Marty Knight was a man who had never come to terms with his past. Until he did, he could have no real future. Oh, yes, she could give him her love and her support. But they'd never be enough to relieve him of what Lydia Foster had once called his emotional baggage. Never. Ever.

Some bad things have happened to you in your life, Donna, a wise man had said to her on what she'd come to think of as the first day of her second life. *I won't try to tell you they haven't. And you aren't to blame for them. But you* are *responsible for what you do about them. The past can be quicksand if you let it. It can be a firm foundation for the future, too. It's up to you.*

"Donna?" Trish questioned, her smoky violet eyes anxious.

Donna sought for the right words. She found them in the echoes of something the beautiful showgirl who'd once been called Fatsy Patsy had said a short time before.

"I would if I thought I could help," she replied. "But I don't think my going to Vegas will help Marty."

Thirteen

As Donna let herself into her house the following Monday evening she heard her recorded voice saying, "... and a message, and I'll get back to you as soon as I can."

She'd gone to work, as usual, that morning. But directly after the weekly staff meeting, Lydia Foster had told her to take the day off.

"Do you have any idea how you look?" her friend and supervisor had demanded, hands on hips, dark eyes flashing.

"Well, I did catch a glimpse or two in the mirror while I was combing my hair," she'd tried to joke.

Lydia had not been amused. "I want you to take the day off."

"I've got work to do!"

"It'll keep."

"But—"

"Donna. Don't you think the kids know there's something wrong? Last week, I had at least a half dozen of my counselees ask me if you were sick—or mad at them."

Donna had been horrified. "Oh, Lydia—no!"

"Oh, Donna, yes. Now, I know you're hurting. And we're good enough friends so I don't have to pretend I don't know why—even though you won't talk about it. I want you to take a break, all right? Go shopping. Go to a movie. Go home, take a three-hour bubble bath and watch soap operas while you pig out on a quart of buttercrunch ice cream. Just go!"

And so, Donna had.

She'd gone shopping, but she hadn't purchased anything.

She'd gone to a movie, but she couldn't remember a frame of the Oscar-winning epic she'd paid to see.

Now she was coming home to—

BEEP!

"Donna?" Donna froze. The voice was Lydia Foster's and it was frayed to the point of being frantic. "God, girl, where are you? Listen, it's now, uh—"

Donna streaked across the room and snatched the phone out of its cradle.

"Lydia? Lydia?" she asked. Her mouth was dry, her heart was hammering. She'd never, ever, heard Lydia Foster sound so shaken up.

"Donna?"

"Yes?"

"Where have you been?"

"Never mind that! What's wrong?"

"Sam Collins has run away."

"What?"

"They released his father from jail this morning—"

"But that wasn't supposed to happen until Wednesday!"

"I know. I know. There was some kind of paperwork screw-up or something. But the guy got out and the first thing he did was head for a bar."

"Oh, no!"

"The second thing he did was get in a car. Dead drunk. He's not drunk anymore, though. He's just dead. He plowed into an embankment."

Donna closed her eyes. "Oh, God."

"The police showed up here. Apparently one of the kids overheard them talking to me and went and told Sam. By the time I went to find him, he was gone," Lydia reported.

Donna opened her eyes. She allowed herself one hideous moment of guilt, then shoved the emotion aside. Feeling guilty wasn't going to help Sam one bit.

"How long ago?" she asked.

"Hours."

"Are the police looking for him?"

"Yes. And all the staffers we can spare. There's no trace of him."

Donna took a deep breath. "Have you, have you tried to contact Marty Knight?" she asked. She knew he was back from Las Vegas. Her father had informed her of this fact the evening before. She'd had a call from Trish Wren, as well. The awareness that Marty had returned to L.A. had kept her tossing and turning all night. That was one reason she'd looked so dreadful when she'd come to work. "Sam opened up to him a lot. Marty may have some idea where he might have run off to."

There was an odd silence on the other end.

"I've already phoned his house at the beach," Lydia replied after a second or two. "No answer. I left a message on his machine."

Donna wondered fleetingly how Lydia had gotten Marty's home number. She swept her curiosity aside as ruthlessly as she'd pushed the guilt away.

"I'll try a few other places," she said steadily. "Then I'll come to the Center."

After a minute of digging through the contents of the capacious tote bag she carried to and from work, Donna located the paper on which she'd taken down the list of telephone numbers Zeke Peters had given her nearly two months before.

The first call she made was to Marty's house at the beach, just in case. She didn't need the paper to dial that number. She knew it by heart.

No answer. The sound of Marty's recorded voice when the answering machine clicked on made her tremble.

Like Lydia, she left a message.

Ignoring the numbers related to his work on *Murphy's Law,* she tried the one marked Manager.

A busy signal.

Finally she tried his car phone.

Please, oh, please, she thought.

"Hello?"

"M-Marty?"

"Donna? Donna? Is that you?"

"Yes."

"Are you all right?"

"No. I—Sam Collins's father is dead. Sam's run away!"

Marty swore. "Are you at the Center?"

"No, I'm at my house. I was just—"

"Hang up and stay put, sweetheart. I'll be there in less than ten minutes."

"Nothing!" Donna said in a half angry, half anguished tone about five hours later. She and Marty had spent most of that time driving the streets around the Center. Not once had they mentioned what had happened in Las Vegas nine days before. When they'd spoken, which hadn't been very often, it had been about Sam.

"We're going to find him, Donna," Marty replied.

"If anything's happened to him..."

"It hasn't!" came the fierce response. "And it won't. Sam's a tough kid."

"But he's just a little boy! He doesn't have any money. He doesn't have any family. It's after dark..." God. Oh, God. She suddenly wished she were a little less aware of how dangerous a place the world could be for children.

"We're going to find him," Marty repeated, shifting gears. Then, very deliberately, he reached over and covered Donna's left hand with his right. He slanted her a glance and squeezed, once. Then he let go of her hand and returned his gaze to the road.

Donna sat in trembling silence, dizzyingly aware that it had been close to three weeks since Marty had touched her. She'd noticed that he'd been very careful to keep his hands to himself when he'd arrived at her house less than eight minutes after he'd hung up his car phone. There'd been a split second, when they'd first looked into each other's eyes, when she'd thought he was going to close the distance between them and embrace her, but nothing had happened.

She'd noticed a lot besides Marty's avoidance of physical contact during the past hours. There was something...different...about him. For all his obvious concern about Sam—and her—he radiated a new sense of assurance. The turmoil she'd felt in the days before his departure for Las Vegas was gone. Yes, there was a definite reticence toward her, but even that restraint had a kind of certainty about it.

"Marty—" she began.

The buzz of his car phone interrupted her. Marty scooped it up.

"Yeah?" he said. "Yeah—*what?* When? Is he okay? Wha— Are you sure? No. *No!* Call them back and tell them we're on our way." He hung up and flicked on the turn signal.

"Marty?"

He looked at her. As dark as it was, she caught what looked like a sheen of tears in his compelling eyes. "That was my manager, sweetheart. The police called him. Somebody tried to break into my house."

Donna pressed her fingers against her lips for an instant. "S-Sam?"

"Yeah. The cops have him at the local station house."

"Is he all right?"

"If he isn't, he will be."

"We found this on him," one of the uniformed officers who'd picked Sam up said. The "this" was a dog-eared page from a magazine. One side of the page bore a photograph of Marty's house, the other part of an interview in which he talked about the joys of living at the beach.

"My God," Donna gasped, taking the page. "This is how he knew?"

"Apparently," the cop said, nodding. "About all he's told us is that some *dude* gave him a ride to the right area, and then he started walking around till he found the house that matched this picture.''

"Tough and smart," Marty murmured.

They came to a halt outside a closed door. "This is one of our interrogation rooms," the officer explained. "We put him in here while we waited for somebody from juvey or child welfare to show up. But now that you folks are here—" He paused. "The kid—what did you say his name was, again?"

"Sam," Marty answered immediately.

"Sam Collins," Donna supplied simultaneously.

"Yeah. Well, Sam seems to be okay physically. He's tired and grubby and he may be hungry, although he hasn't eaten anything we've given him. But emotionally..." The cop shook his head, then opened the door.

Sam was sitting at a small table placed in the middle of the room. His head was down and he had his arms wrapped across his upper body. He didn't look up as the door opened but the young policewoman who was sitting at the table with him did. Donna saw her eyes widen in surprised recognition.

"I hear you dropped in to see me, Sam," Marty said quietly.

The youngster's head snapped up. His face was pale and smudged with dirt. His brown eyes were bleak with misery.

"I—I killed my dad," he confessed in a small voice, staring at Marty.

Donna sucked in her breath, realizing instantly what the little boy meant. "No, Sam—"

The child shifted his gaze to her. "I d-did," he insisted, hugging himself even more tightly. "I—I hated him and I wanted him to be dead and now he is. So—so, I killed him. I made it happen. It's my fault."

Marty moved forward and knelt down by the boy. "No," he said, shaking his head. "No. *It's not your fault.*"

"Yes, s-sir."

"No, sir. Your dad was drunk, Sam. He was drunk and he ran his car into a wall. You didn't have anything to do with it!"

Sam's face contorted. "Yes!" he said shrilly. "Yes, I did!"

Marty decided it was time to push. "How, Sam?"

"Because I hated him."

"Why?"

"Because, because—" a giant sob erupted from the little boy. "Because he did what you just said. Because he got drunk and then, and then he hit me. But I never told. *I never told.* I said I wanted to be with him. To be his b-boy. But I didn't! I d-d-d-didn't—"

At this point, Sam threw himself into Marty's arms. Donna's eyes filled with tears as she watched the man she loved embrace the boy he so obviously understood. She heard a suspiciously choky sound from the officer standing next to her and saw the young policewoman blink rapidly several times in a row.

"It's okay," Marty said. "It's okay. I've got you. You're safe. It's good to tell, Sam."

"N-no," Sam wept. "N-n-no."

"Yes."

"You d-don't . . . you don't kn-know."

Donna saw Marty draw a deep breath. Then he angled his head so he could look directly at her. The love she'd seen in his eyes the morning she'd confessed her most closely guarded secret was there again. Yet it wasn't the same. It was warmer and wiser.

"Yes, Sam," he said quietly. "I do."

The boy gulped several times, then disengaged himself slightly from Marty's embrace. He stared at Marty with anguished eyes, tears streaming down his face. "H-how?"

"Because my father use to get drunk and hit me, too."

Sam shudderd. "Were you . . . were you b-bad?"

"I used to think so, buddy, yeah," Marty answered. "I used to think it was my fault my dad drank. I used to think it was my fault he hit me. And . . . it got to the point where I didn't even need a reason to think it."

"R-really?" Sam's gaze flicked back and forth, back and forth.

"Really."

"B-but—" The child's face contorted again. "If I . . . if I wasn't b-bad, how come . . . how come my d-dad said I w-was? How c-come he h-hit me?"

Donna moved forward. "Because he had a sickness, Sam," she said. "His sickness was drinking. But it had nothing—*nothing*—to do with you." She knelt down so her face was level with the child's. "It was *his* sickness. You didn't cause it. And you didn't kill him."

Sam stared at her. "But . . . I w-wanted him to b-be dead."

"It's not the same thing. I swear to you, Sam. What happened to your father was not your fault."

"And what you feel about him isn't wrong," Marty picked up. "He hit you. He called you bad when you knew you weren't. Even now, it's okay for you to feel angry about that. It's more than okay. It's *right*. But you can't hang on to that anger forever. You've got to let it go after a while."

"H-how?"

"Telling helps. Not keeping everything locked up inside."

"But . . ." Sam darted a look at Donna. She nodded encouragingly. "I l-lied to you, M-Miss Day," he said. "All that . . . all that stuff—"

"It's all right, Sam," she told him. She reached out and stroked his shoulder. "I understand."

The little boy turned his eyes back toward Marty. "Telling's h-hard," he said tremulously.

Marty hugged him again. His gaze locked with Donna's. "I know, Sam," he said. "I know how hard it is. But if you don't let the bad stuff out, there's no room to let the good stuff in."

"Is he asleep?" Donna asked several hours later when Marty walked out onto the deck of his house. The glow of the moon and the light from the house made it possible for her to see him quite clearly despite the lateness of the hour.

He nodded. "I'm glad Lydia said it was okay to bring him here."

"She wants what's best for him."

"Yeah." Marty stretched as if trying to unknot his spine. He was wearing nothing but a pair of jeans. Donna felt a fluttering low in her body as she watched the play of the muscles of his torso. Then, suddenly, she frowned. Something was missing ...

"Where's your medallion?" she asked anxiously, taking a step forward.

Marty stopped stretching. He met her questioning gaze steadily. "I gave it to Sam. For the times he needs a special reminder that there's somebody who really cares about him."

Donna moistened her lips. She caught a flare of response in Marty's dark eyes. A little tremor went through her. "You ... you don't need a special reminder anymore?"

Marty didn't say anything.

Donna lifted her chin a notch. Her pulse had accelerated. "I know what happened in Las Vegas," she told him after several seconds.

Marty didn't look away. "Trish told me she came to see you."

"Knowing what happened doesn't mean knowing why, Marty."

His sensually shaped mouth twisted. "Tell me about it." He paused for a moment or two, obviously seeking the right words. Donna stayed silent.

Waiting.

Hoping.

Loving.

Finally he began.

"It's all pretty twisted," he said. "I'm just beginning to see that. But ... part of the *why* is that you were the third person in my life to say you loved me. The first was my mother. The second was my father. He hurt me. She let me be hurt. So something inside me got the message that anyone who said 'I love you' to me was just setting me up to be knocked down."

"Oh, Marty."

"I told you it was twisted. And ... the other part of the why is just as bad."

"Like father, like son."

He nodded. "I was afraid I'd hurt you, Donna. Maybe not physically. But there are worse things than physical pain. We both know that. So I—I..." He gestured.

Donna took a step toward him. She was almost within touching distance. "Didn't you think finding you in bed with another woman would hurt me?" she asked.

He grimaced and raked a hand back through his hair. "I thought it would make you hate me enough to forget the hurt," he answered. "I thought I wanted you to stop loving me."

Donna shook her head. *"Never,"* she told him huskily. "Never in a million years."

Marty drew a shuddery breath. "I broke down in Vegas," he confessed. "After you'd gone. After I'd told Trish to get out. I broke down and cried like a little kid. And once I finished crying, I called Lydia Foster."

Donna's eyes widened. She suddenly remembered Lydia's odd manner the Monday after she'd returned from Las Vegas. She also recalled the fact that her friend had had Marty's home telephone number.

"I told her I needed help," Marty declared bluntly. "And I asked her if she could recommend someone I could talk to about it. She said she could and I took her recommendation."

"Oh, oh, Marty."

He closed the distance between them. He took her in his arms and he gazed down into her eyes. "I've been screwed up about a lot of things for a long time, sweetheart," he said. "And if talking to someone was all it took to get unscrewed up...I'd be fine right now. But being willing to talk is only the first step. I know I've got a long way to go..."

Marty's voice trailed into silence. He shook his head and smiled crookedly. Donna lifted her right hand to his left cheek. He turned his face and kissed her palm.

"There's one thing I've never been screwed up about," he finally went on. "And that one thing is that I love you, Donna Day. I love you with all my heart."

"I love you the same way, Marty Knight," she assured him.

Many kisses later, he eased away from her just a little. Donna heard herself make a throaty sound of protest. The protest died when the man she loved began to speak.

"How would you feel about marrying a younger man?" he asked.

She blinked, wondering if passion had addled her brain. "Y-younger—?"

Marty nodded and smiled a smile that made her bones melt. "You say you were reborn about twelve years ago. Well, by my reckoning, I only went through the process ten days ago. So that makes me—"

"Yes!" Donna cried joyously. "Yes. I'll marry you!"

Donna Elizabeth Day and Marty Knight were married six weeks later.

Donna was given in marriage by her father, who confided that becoming an adoptive grandfather would make up for the loss of his status as the funniest man in his daughter's life. She was attended by her dear old friend, Dr. Lydia Foster, and a new one, Ms. Trish Wren—formerly "Fatsy Patsy" Wrzesniewski of St. Cecilia's in Chicago.

Ms. Wren, the groom later informed his blushing bride, seemed to have a remarkably salutary effect on one of their guests. Arnold Golding—sans girlfriend—had taken one look at her and stopped sneezing.

Marty's best man was Zeke Peters, who discharged his duties with suitable pomp and a minimum of profanity. His one brief slip—a temporary misplacement of the rings—was deftly covered by the happy couple's soon-to-be-adopted son, Samuel Mark Collins.

Neither the bride nor the groom took their vows as innocents or dewy-eyed idealists. They swore to love, honor and cherish as people who had traveled a hard road out of the past alone and who were prepared to face the rocky trail into the future together.

Standing in the sunlight of a perfect morning, Day became Knight . . . and it was wonderful.

* * * * *

From the popular author of the bestselling title
DUNCAN'S BRIDE (Intimate Moments #349)
comes the

LINDA HOWARD

COLLECTION

Two exquisite collector's editions that contain four of
Linda Howard's early passionate love stories. To add
these special volumes to your own library, be sure
to look for:

VOLUME ONE: *Midnight Rainbow*
               Diamond Bay
               (Available in March)

VOLUME TWO: *Heartbreaker*
               White Lies
               (Available in April)

 *Silhouette Books*®

SLH92

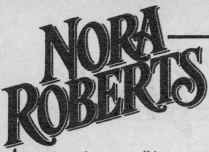